GOLD
UNICORN

Books in the Dragonflight Series

GOLD UNICORN

Tanith Lee

Illustrated by
MARK ZUG

A Byron Preiss Book

Atheneum   1994   New York

Maxwell Macmillan Canada
Toronto

Maxwell Macmillan International
New York   Oxford   Singapore   Sydney

GOLD UNICORN
Dragonflight Books

Cover painting by Mark Zug. Cover design by Brad Foltz.
Edited by John Betancourt

Special thanks to Jonathan Lanman, Keith R.A. DeCandido, and Howard Kaplan.

Atheneum
Macmillan Publishing Company
866 Third Avenue
New York, NY 10022

Maxwell Macmillan Canada, Inc.
1200 Eglinton Avenue East
Suite 200
Don Mills, Ontario M3C 3N1

Macmillan Publishing Company is part of the Maxwell Communication Group of Companies.

First edition
Printed in the United States of America
10 9 8 7 6 5 4 3 2 1

ISBN 0-689-31814-6
Library of Congress Catalog Card Number: 94-71056

To John Kaiine,
My Husband and Good Angel.

FOREWORD

(The Story as Told in Book One: Black Unicorn)

Sixteen-year-old Tanaquil, the red-haired daughter of the red-haired sorceress Jaive, lives with her mother in a fortress in the desert. Tanaquil wants to leave. Her mother's spells cause constant havoc, and besides, Jaive has little time for her. Tanaquil has never even been able to find out who her father was.

Around the fortress live desert animals called peeves, which, due to spillages of Jaive's magic, have learned to talk. One of these peeves unearths a collection of beautiful bones, which Tanaquil—who has no apparent talent for sorcery, but can mend things—fixes together. She discovers these form the skeleton of a unicorn. One night the unicorn puts on flesh and comes alive, a black beast with a glimmering, starry horn. It leads Tanaquil—and the peeve—away into the desert.

Alternately helped and hindered by the unicorn, Tanaquil crosses the desert and reaches a large exotic city by the sea. Here she meets Lizra, the daughter of the city's ruler, and next the ruler himself, the cold, difficult Prince Zorander, and his evil counselor Gasb. Tanaquil learns that Zorander is her father, and Lizra, therefore, her half-sister.

The city has a legend of a fabulous unicorn, and during a procession to celebrate this beast, the real unicorn appears, disrupting everything and attacking Prince Zorander. It steals from him two white fossils.

Tanaquil has realized that the unicorn is a creature of another world, finer than her own. It wishes only to return there, and she can help it by mending the sorcerous gate-between-worlds, which she has found in the cliffs beside the sea. Tanaquil mends the gate, using the fossils as keys, and the unicorn goes through. But the peeve follows it, and so Tanaquil must follow too.

The unicorn's world is the Perfect World, putting Tanaquil's to shame. Everything there is beautiful, balanced, peaceful, good. To her horror Tanaquil sees that her mere presence can wound this perfection, and so she prepares to leave. Before she does so, the unicorn touches her, and the peeve, with its starry horn.

Back in her own world, Tanaquil destroys the gate and keeps the fossils to safeguard the unicorn's country. When Gasb presently attempts to have her killed, Tanaquil learns that the unicorn has made both her and the peeve safe from physical danger—they are invulnerable.

She must now face up to the fact that she is, with her incredible knack of mending, in her own way a sorceress. And the peeve is her familiar.

Gasb has been murdered, and Zorander has become sickly and weak after the unicorn's assault. Lizra declares that she must stay with her father. Tanaquil, however, sets out with the peeve, on her travels, to see her own world, of which she knows so little. She sends a letter to her mother, promising that she will come back . . .

GOLD
UNICORN

PART
One

I

Tanaquil's mind was on higher things: the three flights of stairs that still lay ahead of her. She, along with the others, had already climbed four flights. Four was more than enough. Especially after all the coins they had had to leave at the door.

Lady Mallow leaned on Lord Ulp, gasping.

The rest of the nobles panted, and, where they had breath, complained.

The only one who had had no trouble with the endless stairs was the peeve, which had sprinted up each flight, tugging at the leash, and nearly pulling Tanaquil over. Various people had been tripped up by the peeve, and presently Tanaquil heard a penetrating plummy male voice announce, "Why has this woman's animal been let in, when we were told all our servants must be left downstairs?" Nobody replied, except for the peeve, which said, "Rrrh." It usually obeyed Tanaquil and remembered not to speak in front of strangers.

Lady Mallow now said, "The magician inflicts this climb out of malice."

"You would come," said Lord Ulp.

They went on, painfully, up the fifth stair.

In their hands the lighted candles they had been given by the coin-collecting black-robed attendants below flickered and smoked. No other lights burned in the stone house of Worabex.

"Thank the God we didn't bring your mother," panted Ulp, as they got on to the sixth flight.

"She would have refused to come up," said Lady Mallow. "Tanaquil, dear, are you managing?"

"Yes, thanks."

"And the dear animal?"

The dear animal chose this moment to rush ahead again and Tanaquil, with a curse and an apology, was dragged past Ulp and Mallow, past a corpulent old noble with a stick—which he waved—and so into the breathless lead.

"Peeve—stop it—sit!"

"*Things!*" hoarsely squealed the peeve, forgetting it was supposed to be a dog, speechless and normal.

Tanaquil had no breath to protest further. She thought of letting go the leash—as she had thought of letting it go so many times through the last year, on her travels. The day, for example, when the peeve chased a small rhinoceros through the market of North City, or when it decided the puppets of the puppet show (in a large town called Glop) were really rats. But, now as then, she did not dare. There might be anything at the top of the stairs. Worabex was supposedly a great magician, and that was why Lord Ulp and Lady Mallow had brought her here. Perhaps the peeve, born in the house of a sorceress, had missed the smells of magic.

On the last flight, in any case, Tanaquil lost her balance, and the leash ran out of her hand.

"Come *back!*"

Useless, of course.

In the candle-fluttering dimness of the hot summer twilight, Tanaquil watched the peeve shoot up twenty final stairs and vanish in at a large, dark, vaulted doorway.

There followed a loud crash, a bang, a sound like china plates falling, and then a flash of white that lit up everything in a weird and uninformative way.

Next moment the peeve hurtled out again. It leaped at Tanaquil, and clung to her leg, clawing at her only good dress. "Mistake," said the peeve.

"Oh, hell," said Tanaquil.

Behind her, one of the ladies tut-tutted. At the moment it was thought very unlucky to swear.

Everyone waited. Then, from within the shadowy door, a voice boomed out.

"Which of you owns the animal?"

"I do," said Tanaquil. "I'm sorry."

"It must be tied up."

"Don't want," said the peeve.

"Too bad, I'm afraid."

Tanaquil tied the peeve to the banister rail, which was carved to resemble a rearing serpent. The peeve, fortunately, did not notice. It hissed and spuffed under its breath.

The other people who had come to visit the great magician Worabex had now reached the last landing. They assembled, puffing and uneasy.

"You may enter," the voice boomed. "All but the animal."

The peeve sat down dejectedly. Moving so much in the human world, it had almost learned when No meant No.

As the group of nobles trod cautiously in at the doorway, a soft light bloomed.

Tanaquil, the last to enter, darted a glance around. There were certainly strange things in the vast chamber, but she could see no actual damage. Perhaps the peeve had breached a spell—which was probably much worse.

The walls ascended into a vast dome, and in this dome hung a black crocodile on a brass chain, slowly circling there in a mysterious air current. One of its legs twitched. A lady squeaked.

"There is nothing to fear," said the voice. It was smug, Tanaquil thought. They were meant to be terrified.

Worabex himself was not visible, but among the groups of tall black chests, machineries, and implements of iron and silver suspended from the ceiling was a large oval mirror. Into this an enormous mouth abruptly loomed. It was greenish, with long yellow teeth. It caused more squeaks and exclamations. Tanaquil was not impressed. Her own mother had been prone to such manifestations, although to some extent Jaive had grown out of them. Not Worabex, apparently.

"Welcome," said the green mouth, "to my sorcerium. There is no need to be afraid, provided you do as I recommend. What did you wish to see?"

The fat old noble with the stick lurched forward. "Do you have something to deal with the enemy? With the Mad Empress Veriam, who devours children and destroys the land?"

"Oh, the war," said the mouth. "The matter has been put to me. I have listened."

"Goody," muttered Tanaquil. The magician, as she had known he would, irritated her extremely. Was that why she had come? To prove to herself how irritating magicians were?

One of the walls behind the engines briefly dissolved. Blue and glycerine, a dragon uncoiled itself in a cave of fires. Or seemed to.

Two of the noble ladies attempted to faint. The dragon winked out.

The fat old noble said, tetchy, "Is that your answer, Worabex?"

The mouth also vanished from the mirror. For a startling moment it was ordinary glass, and Tanaquil saw her own self reflected there. She had not glimpsed herself for months, save in the warped copper mirrors Lady Mallow favored—she had sadly explained this reflection was kinder as you got older. Now Tanaquil saw a girl of seventeen, slim and strong, in her best dress, which was based on a "country" style, and not boned at the waist. The material was a nice brown, embroidered with iris color, and with a broad, beaded light red sash that matched her hair. The peeve had clawed a hole about three inches above the left ankle.

Tanaquil shook her head, and from her ears swung the two white earrings she always wore.

Then that image too was gone. Instead of the mirror, the magician Worabex had arrived. He was of unamazing appearance, rather bald, and with a thin mouth that was not green. He wore a black robe with gold snakes on the sleeves. These sleeves seemed to annoy him slightly. He had obviously put the garment on to impress his audience.

"You doubt me," said Worabex. It was neither a question nor a statement.

The old fat noble said, leaning on his stick, "I asked what weapons you had created for tackling the Empress-Enemy. The woman who makes war on us."

Worabex said, "After all, she doesn't really want to make war. She only wants to conquer the land." The fat noble offered a noise. Worabex said, "Obviously, it's possible to stop any war. But five minutes later, the war, or another war, would start again. Human nature needs to be changed. That is the key."

The fat old noble swore, inventively, and the ladies let out quacks of distress. Another lady "fainted."

The fat noble said, "I'll be frank. I'm scared. At my age you don't want all this trouble. Conquering hordes and so on. Make me young again. I'll fight the Empress's soldiers. I'll be brave."

"I could make you young, of course," said Worabex.

"Humph. Being young isn't so wonderful." The fat noble considered. He said, "I recollect, being young hurt. So does old age. Just you get rid of the Warrior Empress."

Tanaquil watched Worabex look round at all of them, and at last his black eyes came to rest on her. She gazed modestly down at her sandals.

"And you are the girl with the animal."

"I tied it to the banister," said Tanaquil quickly.

"Yes, but what do you think of all this?"

"It's ever so lovely," minced Tanaquil. "*Awesome!*"

The magician cleared his throat. "I meant, the war with the Empress."

"I don't know much about it," said Tanaquil. "I've been traveling. I heard rumors. And then I got here and heard rather more. She's conquered three or four countries and wants this one as well. Is that it?"

"You don't seem anxious," said Worabex.

"I am, in one way. I have—relatives who may live in one of the conquered zones." Tanaquil wondered why she had said so much. Perhaps the abominably smug magician was practicing on her, loosening her tongue. She added in a flattering tweet, "But then, I'm only a woman. What would *I* know?"

The magician Worabex gave a laugh.

He said, "Usually, when people come to my house, I am expected to entertain *them*. However, I have enjoyed your performance. Maybe you would all like to see a swarm I've made?"

"A secret weapon," declared another of the nobles.

"Conceivably," amended Worabex.

Worabex raised his arm and a black curtain rose from an archway. Smooth, pale light came up beyond, showing a bizarre sort of indoor zoo. Tanaquil recalled her mother's collection of mice and cats, whom she used regularly to turn into other things, or whom she would "improve," adding long ears or tails, odd colors, and so on. The animals had seemed happily indifferent, but Tanaquil thought the procedure wrong.

The beasts in the magician's enclosure were of this sort, too. A large turquoise dog sat on some cushions, gnawing a bone—Tanaquil was glad the peeve had been left outside. Dangerous-looking fanged carp swam in a tank, and in another place small red lions, about the size of squirrels, were playing with a ball.

Worabex indicated a golden shutter let into the wall. He spoke a word, and the shutter flew up. There behind, in a big glass orb, some striped things were flying busily about. They buzzed.

The nobles peered.

There was an air of disappointment and disbelief.

"You are contemptuous of us, Worabex!"

Intrigued despite herself, Tanaquil craned to see.

She burst into a sharp, loud laugh.

"Oh, good," said Worabex. "I have amused you in turn."

"Flying mice," said Tanaquil.

"Somewhat more. Only somewhat, naturally."

In the orb, the ten or so creatures settled on a potted bush and began to preen themselves. They were certainly mice, each with large wings like those of a giant dragonfly. Their fur was black, with broad yellow stripes.

"A crossbreed," said Worabex.

Lady Mallow went forward and stroked the glass. "How lovely. Would we be able to purchase a couple?"

"You must understand," said Worabex, "that although I charge an entrance fee to my house, I sell nothing. Besides, I'm not sure you would really want these beasts in your home."

Just then, one of the animals flew up again and lashed out, with its long mouse tail, at the side of the orb where Mallow's fingers were. Mallow gave a small scream. Something dripped nastily down the inside of the glass.

"I call them," said Worabex, "mousps. They are a mixture of mouse and wasp, and have a sting in the tail."

There was some murmuring.

Tanaquil thought, The silly mixed with the vicious. Is that what Worabex is too?

Before she had time for further reflection, beyond the two chambers, in the direction of the stairs, came a peculiar scrabbling and worrying sound, followed suddenly by an enormous thump and crack.

Tanaquil turned in time to see a bundle of fur and splinters erupting into the sorcerium. It was the peeve tangled up in its leash, kicking and biting and fighting the serpent carving from the banister.

The magician looked surprised. Everyone else shouted. Including Tanaquil, who also ran forward.

The battling peeve, however, had already cannoned into one of the sorcerous machineries, which surged into wild life, sending out green rays and chugging. "Bite! Bite!" snarled the peeve, rolling now into a cabinet, which rocked. The doors flew open and some books flew out, literally flew on broad wings.

The nobles ducked in alarm as the flock of books dived over, and Worabex said, "I give you ten seconds to catch your animal, young woman."

Tanaquil flung herself on the peeve and was pulled into a hanging disk of bronze which gave off a twanging tone and emitted a hail of hard red lights. From the corner of her eye, she saw the turquoise dog rising interestedly.

Then the ten seconds were presumably up, for a terrible noiseless thunderclap passed over them all, leaving them stunned, so even the peeve uncurled and lay panting, staring about with huge yellow eyes. "Moon," said the peeve undecidedly.

"Yes, it's the moon. He's thrown us out. Truly thrown us. Magically."

One of the ladies really had fainted and was being bent over by another with a bottle of reviving salts. The rest of the company stood gaping on the bare and unpromising cliff, the mile-high top of which they now occupied.

The peeve sat up and pawed the carved serpent. "Killed it," said the peeve virtuously, not expecting to be thanked.

II

It's all right," said Tanaquil. "Look, there's the road down there. And I can make out the carriages and horses and the torches of your servants."

"Just answer this," said the old fat noble, "how do we get down?"

Tanaquil had no reply. She had already apologized for the peeve, wondering grimly as she did so if this was apology three million and six or three million and seven.

The lady who had fainted said to Lady Mallow shakily, "It's a nice view, isn't it? You can see such a long way." And fainted again.

"Lost her mind from the shock," said the fat noble, congratulatory.

"It wasn't Lady Tanaquil's fault," said Lord Ulp. "Just that damnable rat-dog-thing of hers."

The peeve said, "Not rat. *Bite* rat. *Bit* snake."

Nobody heard.

Lady Mallow said, "I think Worabex behaved most unfairly."

"Better not say so," said Ulp. "God knows what'll happen next."

But nothing happened. And dimly below—perhaps the cliff was not quite a mile high—they saw the servants signaling with their torches and heard vague, encouraging shouts.

"Turned some fellow into a duck, I heard," said the fat noble. He added, "Couldn't make me young again though, could he?"

Tanaquil felt the impatience that sometimes came when she

was with people so much older than herself. She supposed her mother, who had nearly always made her impatient, was the root cause of this feeling.

It was going back to see her mother, in order to keep her promise to her mother that she *would* go back, that had put Tanaquil, indirectly, into this position.

Tanaquil, who had seen a great deal in her year of travel, had managed so far to avoid the war zones of the rumored Empress called Veriam. Then she found herself coming out of the forests and onto a road that ran between great golden towering fields of wheat and corn. The camel, which she had kept despite the changes of terrain, was pleased with the fields and sometimes browsed on them. There seemed a superabundance. Then a small group of women appeared, working with scythes, and they shouted at the camel furiously.

One ran up and pointed at Tanaquil. "You filthy outlander. You keep that mucky great beast—is it a monster?—out of the wheat! Don't we have misery enough. How can we reap all this alone, with our men all gone? And then, insult to injury, you let that walloping thing chew up the grain."

So then Tanaquil had had to apologize for the camel, which had already withdrawn its disdainful face and stood like a king on the road. The peeve growled, and the woman had shrieked: "And what's that? It's an abomination—are you a spy for the wicked Empress-Enemy?" And then run off howling. All the other women menaced Tanaquil with their scythes, and she put the camel into a fast lope.

When they had escaped, and got back into the edges of the forest, she thought about the encounter. Obviously the missing men had been called up and gone to fight off the Empress.

It was strange in a way. The late summer was lush and beautiful. Birds sang cool as fountains in the woods, and the harvests were early and rich. But there were not enough hands to take them in, with the men gone . . . and soon enough, in a village, Tanaquil saw those men who had come back. The one-legged man and the blinded man, who had lost their limb and eyes in the war. Somehow, as in stories and songs, she expected wars to happen in time of draught or storm, armies trailing over pitiless snow, beneath the wind, or through withered fields. Not like this, with all the plenty wasted.

The day after, Tanaquil met Lord Ulp and Lady Mallow on the road. Their carriage wheel was off and the driver sat at the roadside, saying it was not his place to repair wheels. So Tanaquil mended the wheel, while Lady Mallow fell in love with the peeve, which began to act in an excessively soppy way, pretending to be just what Lady Mallow thought it, a lovely furry barrel of a pet, with a dainty pointed snout and fluffy tail. It kept saying, "Me, *me,*" but Lady Mallow thought this was a sort of doggy meow. Lord Ulp only asked if it had fleas.

Lady Mallow presently invited Tanaquil—or the peeve—to stay with them at their country villa. They had gone there, they said, to avoid the town, which the mad, wicked Empress Veriam might soon lay siege to.

From the talk, Tanaquil finally realized that the wicked Empress had come from the direction in which she was going. (Other information was sparse.) Had Tanaquil's mother therefore been involved in the conquests and war? Had the city by the sea been swallowed up? If it had, was Lizra, her sister, a prisoner? Tanaquil even spared a thought for her princely father, Zorander. Had he died in battle? Did it mean anything to her if he had?

These thoughts bothered Tanaquil. And she was exasperated. It seemed to her she had not been able to leave home for a moment without Jaive and everyone else getting themselves into trouble.

The second day she was at the villa, Lady Mallow suggested Tanaquil would like to visit the magician Worabex. A party of nobles was to go to his house. Perhaps they would learn something there, some prophecy concerning the war and their fates.

Tanaquil had been dubious. But nevertheless she had gone, mostly to please Lady Mallow, who was kind, and seemed to think the jaunt would be exiting for Tanaquil, a treat. Tanaquil had wondered if she herself meant to use the visit as a rehearsal. After all, if she got back to her mother, she would have to deal with all this magic nonsense again. The sorcery and spells and muddles and ridiculous flights of fancy, trick mirrors, rabbits with cat's ears. So, in a way, this too was Jaive's fault. Being here on this cliff in the darkness of the summer night. Jaive's fault and the peeve's.

You *could* see a long way.

The fields glimmered palely under the moon, unreaped. The forests clung black, looking after themselves. And here and there a spoon of water glittered. These were fertile lands, not like the desert where Tanaquil had grown up. Surely, surely, deserts were the place for wars, not country like this—

Something shone faintly red. It was miles and miles away. What was it? Could it be the glow of fires by night, the watch fires of a great army . . . ?

Tanaquil turned from the view, resolved not to draw attention to this possible sign of menace.

Worabex stood beside her. He was more casually dressed and looked even less dramatic than before.

"Oh, hallo," said Tanaquil sweetly. "Can we get down now?"

"In a moment," said Worabex. He said, "You're a very fascinating girl, Tanaquil—it isn't *Lady* Tanaquil, is it?"

"No," said Tanaquil, "Princess, actually. My father was a prince."

"Dear me. Royalty. Well, I get all sorts here."

"Quite," said Tanaquil. She remembered what the peeve had done, and added, "I'm sure we all deserved this. It must be a nuisance for you."

"I need the money," said Worabex. "For my experiments."

"Oh, can't you just magic some up?"

"My dear girl, if I did that, I would wreck the economy."

Tanaquil looked away along the cliff. The party of nobles was somehow very distant. They seemed not to see Worabex, or even herself, anymore. The peeve was sitting in the lap of Lady Mallow, probably saying "Me, *me*."

"I believe," said Worabex, "that you are also acquainted with sorcery. An aunt perhaps."

"Perhaps."

"Your animal talks, of course, and is your familiar. You're something of a sorceress yourself."

"I just mend things," said Tanaquil.

"A useful gift. But there's more. Oh, yes. And you are much traveled. What have you seen worth seeing?"

Tanaquil would have liked to keep quiet, but after all he was a genuine magician and it was better to be polite.

"A tree they claimed was the tallest in the world."

"And was it?"

"It *was* very tall. And I saw a statue in the south that talked and sang."

"These things impressed you."

"It all impressed me. I went to see it because—" she hesitated. "I'd seen somewhere else that was very—beautiful. And I wanted to see the beautiful places here, too. And they are. But usually something spoils things. Disease and poverty and unhappiness. How can you concentrate when you see that?" Tanaquil stopped herself. She was saying too much.

And Worabex said, "I think you must have glimpsed one of the perfect worlds."

"Is there more than one?"

"Several," he said. "And other worlds which are worse."

Tanaquil said, "You've upset the lords and ladies pretty thoroughly. Do you think you should let them get down the cliff now?"

"Presently. I was enjoying our talk."

Tanaquil glanced at Worabex uneasily.

"Yes?" she said brightly.

"I should like to know you better, Tanaquil."

Tanaquil frowned.

On her travels too she had met here and there young men who had said this sort of thing. Now and then she had eaten a meal with one of them, or walked along some shady lane or by some tranquil shore. Nothing else. Now Worabex, who was old and bald, was apparently wanting to court her as the young men had. She had refused *them.* She felt more than ever irritated by the magician.

"I'm ever so sorry," she gushed, "it would be so lovely. But, you see, I'm betrothed to someone. In the north."

Worabex laughed.

"And I am old and boring," he said. "Does it occur to you that once I was your age?"

"And obviously," snapped Tanaquil, "you can make yourself young again, with a spell."

"To conjure up riches would wreck the economy," said Worabex. "Can you imagine the mess it would make of nature if I magicked myself back to nineteen years?"

Tanaquil twittered. "Oh, you're too clever for me."

"And you, my girl, have a great deal to learn about men. How can it be you are so contemptuous of us? You say your father is a prince, but I think you seldom saw him. Failed to like him when you did. There are lessons ahead, Tanaquil."

Tanaquil said, angrily, "There always are."

But Worabex had somehow disappeared, or slipped behind a bush.

The plummy noble was shouting and flapping his arms in the distance.

A flight of stairs had appeared, which led down the cliff.

Tanaquil glanced once over her shoulder. She could no longer see the red glow of far-off fires.

Lady Mallow took the brown dress from her maid and held it up before Tanaquil.

"Ah," sighed Lady Mallow, "once I was slim! But look. They've repaired the hole in the skirt." It was true. The hole had completely gone. "Now, won't you choose a couple of other dresses? There are ten here, and my daughter will never wear them again."

"You're very kind," said Tanaquil, "but I really only need one dress."

Lady Mallow sighed once more. "My daughter, Lavender, married and moved far away from us. We never see her now. She writes once a year, or at festival time. I'm glad of course that she's out of the way of this war. But I remember how close we were. I wonder sometimes if the empress—if Veriam—has a mother. Surely a mother would have talked to her. They say she eats little children! Do you have a mother, my dear?"

"*Oh,* yes," said Tanaquil.

"How she must miss you."

Tanaquil gave a sickly smile.

She had told Lady Mallow she was journeying back toward the

east, because Lady Mallow had been so anxious about Tanaquil riding headlong into the troops of the Mad Empress. In fact, Tanaquil would keep to her original plan. The enemy army must be enormous, and it should be easy to avoid it.

"Do at least take some jewelry. Why not the gold earrings I showed you? Those white ones you wear must be so heavy. Don't they cause a headache? Are they shells?"

"That's right. Strangely enough, they don't weigh anything, or I'm used to them." Tanaquil did not add that the white fossils of her earrings were also the two keys to the gate of another, better world, where war was unknown, cities floated in the sky for winged citizens, lions lay down with lambs, and a unicorn danced on the hills.

She felt sorry for Lady Mallow, who seemed so desperately to want to give her something, as if only that would make Tanaquil remember her. So finally she picked a little silver ring shaped like a snake, and slipped it on her middle finger. Why had the un-friendly Lavender left so much behind? Had she too wanted to get away from her mother?

Dinner was several courses, ending in a huge cheese pie. Lady Mallow fed pieces of ham and cheese to the peeve, which sat on her lap with its ears pointed up, occasionally murmuring, "Me."

However, the moment the meal was over, the peeve leaped down and ran off through the open window to do its nightly tour of the grounds and garden. Faithless, just like Lavender.

In the morning they parted, and Lady Mallow dabbed her eyes. The peeve raced down the path toward the stable, where the camel had been awkwardly housed.

"Do write to me, my dear. I'm so sorry the magician didn't tell you anything."

"There was nothing really I wanted to know. I prefer to find out as I go along."

"That's wise," said Lord Ulp. He gruffly put his arm about his wife. "Cheer up. We'll buy a parrot."

Lady Mallow was pleased, like a little girl. "Oh, could we?"

When she got up on the camel, Tanaquil inspected her posses-sions, the bag of woven feathers that contained her clothes and books, some things the peeve had stolen, whose owners she had not been able to find, and a drinking cup a romantic young man had pressed on her in North City. The peeve struggled with the camel's hump, trying as usual to flatten it. The camel bore with this, wearing its normal expression of royal despair. Over the year the peeve had otherwise grown accustomed to the camel. In wild places it had slept curled into the camel's side.

The camel was a fine sight, too, with patterned hangings and tassels, but not so fine they would be robbed.

They took the road east, and only up among the woods did Tanaquil select another way. The peeve became talkative, telling Tanaquil about the mice and birds of the forest, how many fleas it had caught, what it had had for breakfast. The world was otherwise peaceful, green, and silent but for birdsong and the notes of crickets.

The annoying memory of Worabex came into Tanaquil's mind, with his threat of "lessons."

She had learned, she thought, an important one already. The stubbornness of her world against improvement. Thinking back now, suddenly, on the perfect world that she had glimpsed, the world of the black unicorn with its sea-changing horn, she wondered if the lesson had not been too cruel. She had tried to be hopeful, but with knowledge hope had shrunk. What could ever be done here, this place of unkindness, desertions, and wars?

III

The woods gave way eventually to a luxuriant plain.

In the late afternoon, two days later, Tanaquil halted the camel and looked out across this landscape which, like everything she had seen that year, did not resemble the desert of her childhood.

The green, ripe grasses were in areas heavy with hundreds of scarlet poppies or white, yellow, and purple flowers, so that the rolling plain, in parts, spread into hills that were deep red or snowy, or lakes of gold and mauve. Trees stood, gracious, spreading shade. The sky swept over, mellowing toward sunset.

They rode on leisurely; the peeve was asleep.

Then, as the first traces of pink and crimson began to come up behind the sunken sun, Tanaquil made out something large moving on the dirt road below.

Was it the enemy horde?

She drew the camel over and in under some handy cypresses.

There they waited.

Soon the noise of the advancing multitude began to reach them. A clanking and rumbling, the snorts and squeals of animals, a higher, thinner noise like whistles.

The first division came up on the road that ran beside the trees.

It was not an army. At least, not in the military sense. Carts drawn by weary donkeys, wagons bulging with furniture and made musical by slung pans, kettles, and cauldrons. Men walked, and girls carried babies. The faces of anxious children and old women peered from the sides of wagons and chariots. Dogs barked, and then a herd of cattle came, some lowing because they needed to be milked. Sheep followed, and a flock of geese. A man passed hung with birdcages full of birds, and after him two men hauling their cart themselves, which was laden with tables, baskets, and pots.

Refugees, fleeing from the fighting and the invader. Tanaquil did not need to go over and question them. Instead she stayed immobile under the trees, and so intent were they, these people, on their plight, that they did not spare the camel and rider a glance.

Overhead the sky flamed like the poppies in the grass and shadows ran before the runaways, who had tried to carry with them their houses on their backs.

The whistling cry was the wail of small babies.

When the last stragglers passed, three men leaning on crutches and a fat woman with a sack on her shoulders and a child clinging to her skirt, Tanaquil sat on in the dark, until the dark flowed out and filled up the sky and the road.

A moon rose, looking down as if it did not matter, pure and white, untouched.

They reached a large deserted village an hour after that. How curious it was in the moonlight.

The mounds of the houses with their silver roofs. Not a lamp burning. Not a sound. Here and there a door swung open, or a gate, and on the street lay a smashed jar and a black stream of wine, and nearby a clock that had been dropped and abandoned. When Tanaquil walked close, leading the camel, and with the peeve creeping beside her, the clock was heard to be ticking. How sinister, that usual sound.

"Bad," said the peeve, "want go somewhere else."

The night was warm, and anyway there was no shelter or welcome here.

They moved along the street silently, over the milk-white moon-paving. In a walled garden a doll lay on its face.

Somewhere in the sky, an owl passed.

The peeve stared up, grumbling.

Then, out into the street three shadows stepped, tall and inky, and real as ghosts.

Tanaquil bit back a cry.

She stood stone still, holding the camel's leading rein. The peeve bushed up its tail and dropped its ears, pushing flat to the ground.

"Well," said someone, "a boy with a camel."

"It's a nice camel, too. I've seen them before."

"Could carry things," said the third one.

Tanaquil thought it would be useless to resist. All this time she had never been robbed. Here in the nightmare of the deserted village it was about to happen. Better be helpful.

"Good evening," said Tanaquil.

"Here," said one of the men, "it's a girl."

Confound them. This might be even more unpleasant than robbery. On the other hand . . . perhaps Tanaquil was safe. She had been protected once—would this still happen? She did not really want to try and see.

The middle man came forward down the street, and the others strode after him. He was much taller than they, and slim as a sword. There was a sword in his belt, too. It slid as he moved and caught the moon. She could not see his face, but his hair was long and dark and fell down his back.

Their voices were all young.

The leader with the sword said, "Speak up. What are you doing here?"

"I was left behind," said Tanaquil, "when the others went."

"Rubbish. You're not from this part of the world. Your speech, your clothes, the camel. And what the hell's *that* animal?"

The peeve made a gobbling sound, and Tanaquil, in preference, let go the camel and reached down to grab it—just in time.

"*Bad,*" said the peeve. "Bite."

"Here," said the second man on the left, "it talks."

"Oh no," said Tanaquil. "People are always thinking that. It's got a funny bark."

"Stand up," said the man with the sword. "Good God! Are you a spy, or what?"

"A spy?" simpered Tanaquil. "Oh *no.*"

The man turned slightly, and the moon caught a profile cut with precision by an artist. Then he was darkness again. On Tanaquil the moon fell full.

"If you must have the camel, take it. I haven't got any money."

"Hard luck," said the sword man. "You'll have to come with us. Tell me, is your hair red in daylight?"

"Usually."

His eyebrows went up, she just saw. He said, "You'll definitely have to come with us, then."

Tanaquil's sinking heart plummeted lower. Did they have another of the red-hair-means-a-witch taboos? Presumably they were with the enemy army (so much for avoiding it), and now she was to be their amusement. If she were clever, she might come out of it alive.

She shrugged. "You're in charge."

"How right you are."

The two other men fell in, one on either side. The shortest man took the camel's leading rein. The other sidestepped the peeve nervously.

Tanaquil picked up the peeve and put it round her neck, its paws dangling. "Stay still. Don't do anything. Sit," she added lamely.

The man with the sword turned round, and again she caught a glimpse of his handsome chiseled face.

The shortest man chuckled. "Lucky for us, though, eh, Honj?"

The sword man—Honj?—said, "Wrong again, Turnip. This one is going to the tent of the Empress Veriam."

There was some astonishment, Tanaquil's not the least. The peeve sizzled. *"Quiet."*

"I hope you're suitably honored," Honj said to Tanaquil.

"Oh, very. I've heard she devours captives lightly roasted. Is that to be my destiny?"

"Much worse, I'd think. Oh yes, much."

The ride was quite a long one. These three must have been scouting ahead of the main army. What a misfortune. If she had kept out of the village, she might not have met them. But then, the village had seemed to compel her.

They had horses, these men Turnip, Dodger, and Honj. Honj was evidently the leader. Each of them, on their somber uniform, had a sort of stitched badge, some kind of insect emblem.

They allowed Tanaquil to ride the camel, which ran with the horses over the plain.

Up from the village, and along the roll of the landscape, through veils of trees, down a deserted paved road, with deserted villas scattered by its side, walls overhung by fruit trees, and the fruit dropped ungathered on the ground.

Eventually, a glow of the rim of a low hill, and over the hill, looking down, the image of fires she had seen, or prophetically imagined, when she looked out from Worabex's cliff or house.

She had expected a huge mass of men and pavilions, but this must be some outpost of the main force, for there were only a few hundred there. Enough to be uncomfortable.

They rode down slowly now, and passed through bands of sentries, and then men, sitting dicing and telling jokes at the fires. Then there was a wide lane between the tents, and battle standards stood at intervals. Tanaquil was so disgusted, she did not look at them. The glint of cloth-of-gold and blood red silk went by as she stared straight before her. Cannon on carts appeared, a stockade with horses, and then a huge golden tent bloomed up like a great wild flower that only opened at night.

Torches burned before the tent.

Some soldiers in armor and mail and medals were standing there, and as they approached, Tanaquil heard distinctly the words: "Here comes that devil Honj. What damned mischief now?"

"Keep Red-Hair here," said Honj.

He swung gracefully off his horse and went over to the golden tent. No one stopped him.

Tanaquil resolutely tried to look at no one and nothing. She was unnerved, too furious to be truly frightened, not yet believing what had happened to her. It was like some silly story someone had made up.

Besides, why would an empress want her?

Honj had gone into the tent.

Two of the armored soldiers in medals came and investigated the camel, ignoring Tanaquil. One of them told the other that this was a special type of cow that they had in the west. Its milk was stored in the hump.

"Pph," said the peeve.

Then the tent flap opened again, Tanaquil saw from the tail of her eye.

"Red-Hair, you can get down and come in now. Empress Veriam will see you."

Resigned, boiling, her stomach finally turning over, Tanaquil got off the camel. The peeve slipped down her like a fur cloak and bolted straight in at the tent.

Honj looked after it, doubtful, amused, and Tanaquil quickened her pace.

She walked into the tent as Honj politely held back the flap for her.

Now she had a better look.

The walls were hung with gilded shields, carpets of blue and red silk. Tassels dripped and disks and bells rested lightly, whispering. About a hundred candles burned with a perfumed melting amber light.

The Empress, unmistakable, was sitting in a chair of ebony inset with mosaic and gold rosettes.

Tanaquil caught her breath.

Veriam was a creature made of gold. She wore golden mail, like a man, a heavy golden cloak, a golden helm with a gold mask that covered most of her face. The chin and lower lip of this face were young and pale, but that was all you saw.

A pale hand, clotted by gold mesh and two or three huge rubies, went up in a gesture of command or challenge.

"You should kneel," said the Empress.

"Should I? No one told me."

Tanaquil knelt. Somehow this felt absurd. Not humiliating or alarming, merely daft.

The peeve was burrowing at the foot of the Empress Veriam's magnificent throne-chair. It seemed bewildered but resolute.

"Shall I remove my animal?" said Tanaquil. She found she had spoken to the Empress in a rather bossy manner. She amended swiftly, "Your Highness."

The Empress was alone, or rather, had been alone. Now Honj had come back in and lounged behind Tanaquil in the doorway. He laughed abruptly.

"Hush," said the Empress.

"I'm sorry," said Honj, "but aren't you overdoing it? Or do you want her to swoon with fear?"

"She won't," said the Empress. "That isn't her style."

Tanaquil thought, I've heard her voice before.

Tanaquil said, "The peeve is eating that cushion there. Shall I stop it, or don't you mind?"

"Oh, Tanaquil," said the Empress, "some things don't change."

She knows my name.

The Empress put up her hands and pushed the helmet and mask off her face.

She was sixteen years old, with a long cascade of black hair.

Tanaquil got up, without being asked.

"If it's a game, I don't think much of it," she said. "Lizra."

For the Empress Veriam, conqueror and child-eater, was her sister.

PART

Two

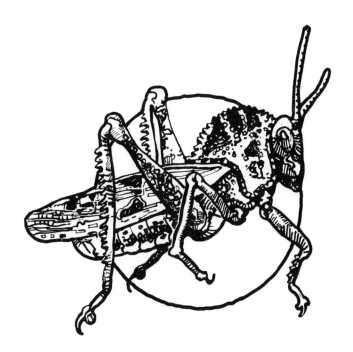

IV

Perhaps it was the largest tent in the world. One of the largest, at least. It seemed to go on and on, rooms leading into rooms through tasseled-secured flaps in the rippling walls of silk and cloth-of-gold, the woven carpets of emerald and magenta. Two of these tent rooms were bathing chambers, with silver baths and gold ewers and jewelry boats to play with in the scented water. One huge room had books and scrolls and other objects of extreme value. There were rooms too for dining and reclining and sleeping and talking and music . . . cushions, instruments, tables, couches. All these things must be packed up every time the army moved. But then the Empress Veriam had a horde of servants to see to it. To make the beds and cool the wines and brew the teas and roast the joints, to shoe the horses of her chariot with gold and silver, and fan her if she were too hot.

"It's my name," said Lizra, throwing a gold disk across the colored board of onyx and pearl, on which she and Tanaquil were trying out a complicated contest. There were boxes of games everywhere too. Like the books and paintings and caskets of gems, they had come from various conquered places. "My name is Lizora Veriam. Lizra's a sort of pet name."

"Your father called you by a pet name?" said Tanaquil. Zorander, their father, had not struck her as that sort of man.

Lizra did not answer. She moved a small castle of aquamarine into position on the board. "Your go."

"I've forgotten what I'm supposed to do."

"Yes, it is rather complicated. Let's stop playing for a while. Have a marinated almond."

"No, thanks. The peeve won't have anymore, either." The peeve, which had roused, lay back on its cushion. It had eaten so much today, and on the previous night after their arrival, that it could hardly move. It burped softly and closed its eyes.

"A sugared grape then? Or these gelatines are good."

"No. Thank you."

"Tanaquil," said Lizra, "you do seem so uncomfortable."

Tanaquil said, "Really?"

"I'm sorry I played that trick on you. I somehow thought I'd told you my formal name before, that you knew, and were pretending too—or that you'd forgotten. I didn't mean to upset you."

"No, that's all right. I mean, I think I did know in some funny way. I was worried about him—Prince Honj. But even that was a joke. He seemed to be joking—but then some men do when they want to cause harm."

"Honj is quite dangerous," said Lizra. She sounded proud. She had, after all, discovered him. "But I'd told him ages ago about you. That I had this feeling you might be traveling in an area where we were. So, you see, you and I *are* close. Even though you went away."

"I didn't go away. I asked you to come with me."

"And you knew I couldn't. I showed you my father, and how he was. I couldn't have left him."

Tanaquil did not reply. She tried to remember the rules of the board game, shook a die of ivory, and cast a disk of platinum. She paused, as if she were thinking, looking at the array of gemstone castles, warriors, ships, chariots, and tiny beasts of quartz and jade.

This was the first time they had been alone. Properly alone, without Lizra's multitude of servants, the blustering captains, and her army of fawning favorites, advisers, the retinue of a great and powerful person. And, of course, Prince Honj, who was nothing of the sort. Like Lizra's former friends—like Tanaquil herself at one point—Honj had been given the title of *prince* to make him more suitable. He had been a wandering mercenary captain from nowhere. He had come to Lizra's army with fifteen men under his command—the "Locusts"—and some cunning notions of how to take various towns, which sometimes worked. He was nineteen years old. Lizra had liked him. Very, very much. So now he was a prince, and the Locusts strutted about, able to do what *they* liked. They had been in the abandoned village, looking for local wine. They had found Tanaquil. And Honj, familiar with Lizra's secrets, recognized her.

Over and over Tanaquil, trying that first night to sleep in one of the glorious sleeping rooms of the tent, had heard Honj's mocking voice: *Tell me, is your hair red in daylight?*

This morning, after the late evening of feasting (in the gold tent), when Tanaquil had sat eating very little and the peeve such a lot, and after her sleepless night, Lizra had had a conference of war with her commanders. Now, this afternoon, here they were, alone. Playing this stupid, too-difficult game.

Lizra seemed at ease, but surely she was not. She had explained nothing. She treated Tanaquil affectionately and—yes, as if she, Lizra, had a right to Tanaquil's presence. Tanaquil did not care for this much. She was not sure what she felt about Lizra herself. *Was* she Lizra anymore? Or only Lizora Veriam, Princess-Ruler of Sea City, Empress of five lands?

"There's a lot I want to ask you," said Tanaquil.

"Naturally. That's why we're alone."

Tanaquil found this faintly patronizing. Lizra was saying, I can predict your needs and have taken care of them. Or was she?

"Well, how did all this happen?"

"What?" said Lizra.

Tanaquil took a deep breath. "That you're an empress. Is it true you're trying to conquer every land from here to the sea? I mean, the other sea . . . the rumors were garbled. Why are you doing it?"

"Oh," said Lizra. She sat back. She smiled. Her face seemed wise and clean and very beautiful. She looked—as if she had seen a vision, something wonderful. Some perfect thing. Like—like the perfect world. "Oh, it's a long tale. And then it isn't. It's the most simple thing on earth. Tanaquil, I'm so glad you're here. I've wanted to talk to you. I used to dream about you, and how I'd tell you everything. But you weren't there."

"I am now."

"Yes. Isn't it good? It was meant to be. I knew I'd find you."

"He found me."

"He found you for *me*."

Tanaquil glanced at the board. She moved a ship of amethyst. She said, "Then tell me about being an empress, Lizra."

Lizra drew up her knees and locked her arms around them. She looked childish, trusting. But her dress was of silver and she wore a jeweled breastplate over it. Tanaquil had already noted the symbol. The symbol of Lizra's army was a unicorn.

Lizra said, "Zorander, my father, is dead. He lived only a month after you—after we parted."

"I'm sorry."

"So am I. He was your father too."

"Yes, but—I didn't ever think of him like that."

"Well. He made it awkward, to be a daughter. And at the end he was demanding and petulant—like a little boy. I felt much older than my father, Tanaquil. And then in the middle of the night, he died. I was asleep. I didn't know till they told me."

Tanaquil sat very quiet. She wondered if she should try to feel some emotion. The idea came to her that one day Jaive, her mother, would die. Would there then, too, be only this uneasy emptiness, this *nothing*?

"It must have been horrible," said Tanaquil. "You must have blamed me. I'd left you. I didn't realize."

"I felt very cold," said Lizra. "It was strange. I'd usually been alone. And now I was."

"Did anyone help?"

"Oh no. It was just the usual formal stuff. Endless processions. The funeral, and everything draped in black and the banners dipped into the dust. And then—they crowned me Prince. You see, if you become the ruler you can't be a woman. So, *Prince* Lizora. I had to wear a dress with so much gold on it I actually couldn't walk. Two grown men had to carry me." Tanaquil grimaced. Lizra said, "And then I had to go out to the people, in the chariot, and with the diadem of the city on my head. It was stormy and hot, and everything weighed on me. But suddenly the crowd cheered. It was a noise I'd never heard."

"They were always cheering you," Tanaquil said.

"Yes. As my father's daughter. But now I was the Prince. The sound—I can't describe the sound. It was like the sea. No, it was like a wave of the world."

Lizra's face was pale and holy.

Tanaquil waited. Finally, she said, "And . . . it changed you."

"Yes, I knew you'd understand. It was that they'd given themselves to me. Into my keeping. I stood between them and God. I don't know if my father ever felt it. More than being a king. Being a *priest*."

Tanaquil listened in her head and tried to hear the sound of cheering as Lizra had heard it. Far, far away, it came to her. The little hairs rose on her neck.

Lizra smiled kindly. "Obviously, it must sound peculiar. You'd have had to be me. Anyway, I knew I'd taken on a special role. And then there was a dispute with a neighboring country, and I took my army, and I fought and I won. And after that I began to see the plan."

"What plan?"

"The great plan. The way to end all unhappiness. To make this world perfect."

Tanaquil had heard of people going white, and now she experienced it happening to her. She could not speak. But she did not need to.

"Now there's no unity. Everyone squabbles with everyone. The way to make it work is to have *one* system for everything. And so you need one rule. Tanaquil, I'm going to conquer the world. I'm going to conquer it and put it right. I recollect—you told me—you'd seen the flawless place behind the magic gate by the sea. Where the unicorn went. Where it had come from. And ours was the unicorn city. It's our emblem. Father had it taken away, and I've put it back. It's on my banner."

"I know."

"I can make *this* world perfect. I can get rid of pain and misery. There'll be a law for everything. My advisers are making them now. No wars—we'll all be one. No illness—because the physicians will all work together to find cures. No envy—everyone will have a proper chance. No poverty. No anger."

"But—," said Tanaquil. She stopped. Lizra had not heard. Tanaquil said, "What about freedom?"

Lizra frowned slightly. "Freedom?"

"You'll be making slaves, won't you? Prisoners and slaves, who have to do what you say."

"I know what to do," said Lizra. "Oh, they'll worry for a while, and then it will be wonderful, and they'll thank me. You see, I have ideas for everything. For example, everyone who is young will dress in pale green."

"Supposing they don't like pale green?" said Tanaquil.

Lizra said, "But they will. And there will be festivals for the young. And then again there will be festivals for older people—"

"What color will *they* wear?"

Lizra laughed. She said, "You look so stern. I'm not explaining properly. It makes me excited. But, Tanaquil—there's something I want you to see. I was going to wait, but that wouldn't be right. I want you to share this with me. And I need your help."

"Surely not."

"Come on. Leave that great fat stuffed peeve. It's fast asleep. Come with me now."

They walked out of the golden tent, and there the scene of the army lay. Apparently the greater force was deployed in three directions, each section less than an hour away. The numbers here were only five hundred. Even so, they were busy. Hammers rang, drums beat, horses were being exercised.

Nearby, on open ground, Prince Honj was drilling his men. They were now a company of twenty-five, all smartly dressed in black, with the Locust badge stitched in gold just below their left shoulders.

Honj turned as Lizra emerged from her tent, and he flung up his arm and bellowed: "The Empress!"

At once all the nearer soldiers shouted and applauded.

Lizra smiled again. Then she smiled at Honj.

He came over on his long legs. He wore a long-billed blue velvet hat, and under it his large eyes were leaden blue, like sky reflected in iron. He looked like no one Tanaquil had ever seen.

"Lady!" said Honj, and dropped faultlessly to one knee.

Lizra giggled. Stopped herself.

"Get up, silly. Your men look nice and fit."

"They are. Shall we raid another village and bring you another sister?"

"This one is quite enough."

Honj looked at Tanaquil. She felt a spark of rage as he doffed his madcap and bowed.

"I'm taking her to see it," said Lizra.

"Indeed."

Lizra walked off over the grass, and the soldiers roared and waved and beat their shields with their fists and knives. Honj had stood up, and as Tanaquil passed, he murmured, "She smiled and her face cracked. Ow, ow." She could have killed him.

There was another huge tent. It was monstrously high, and black. It lay behind lines of men, who rose and shouted as Lizra passed.

The tent was guarded by twenty soldiers, who uncrossed their spears but, businesslike, mechanical, did not shout.

Lizra passed into the tent, and Tanaquil followed.

It was dark after the sunlight on the plain.

Lizra said, "Usually I bring servants and they light the lamps, but I'll do it. I just wanted to bring you here."

Tanaquil thought, Is she trying to flatter me? Make me feel wanted?

But Lizra glided about, lifting a taper she had kindled from a tinderbox, and swinging lamps on brass chains came alight.

There was a mound in the tent. It was a tall mound. A drape of black cloth between twenty and twenty-two feet high. It reminded Tanaquil of something. What—?

Then Tanaquil thought of her mother's hall, and the unicorn running, swathed in curtain, and the bolt of magic—But that was not like this.

Lizra twitched a black silken cord.

The mound of cloth fell, and there—

"What have you done?" said Tanaquil.

"Isn't it magnificent?"

Tanaquil stared. She stared at something she had seen before. But then it had not been like this.

The unicorn stood motionless. It was a giant. Bigger than the elephant she had seen in the south. It was like a wall, or a building. It *shone.* It was, as the Empress had been, a creature of gold. Golden body, articulate and narrow as a greyhound's. Tail of flame. Fetlocks, mane, of spun light. It towered above them, gleaming. And from the body rose the maned slender head, and from the head, whose eyes glowed like scarlet crystal, like *blood,* rose the sun ray of the golden horn.

But it was not real. Not flesh. Not magic.

It was a machine.

For Lizra pointed and said, "It's iron, Tanaquil, plated by gold. And all the joints and wheels and cogs are the finest brass. It moves by lighting a fire in its stomach. The steam makes it *move.* Only—only it doesn't. They can't make it do a thing. We came away from the main army to give our artisans time with it. But they're fools." Tanaquil waited, her heart beating painfully. Lizra said, "It's the symbol of my army, Tanaquil. Of what I want and mean to do. Of conquest. Power. My God-given right to put right the world. And I recall, of *course* I do, how you could mend *anything.* Make anything work. And here you are. Just in the nick of time."

V

No, Lizra was not the same. Or she had become what she had always been. Her father's daughter.

As the shadows of evening began to form, Tanaquil sat on a couch and thought about what had happened. Soon there was going to be another feast. Roast dishes and dishes of baked fruits, and pies and sweets and a hundred other things. Prince Honj would come in with his three lieutenants, Dodger, Turnip, and Mukk. The favorites would come. The captains.

Tomorrow they would be on the march, having rejoined the other three sections of the army. Then it was on to the town—the town from which Lady Mallow and Lord Ulp had fled. Probably a siege, they had been saying casually, oiling the cannons and sharpening their spears.

Lizra had walked Tanaquil round the golden unicorn, showing her its joints and seams, hammered with gilded nails. They had been able to pass *under* the arch of the belly, which had somehow felt quite horrible, perhaps as if it might collapse on them. Lizra had pointed out the panels where things were undone and refueling would take place, hot coals pushed down into the unicorn's brazier-stomach, pipes that received water. Lizra had explained that a platform and short flight of steps would be put up so that Tanaquil could reach the insides of the unicorn, where the cogs and wheels were that would not work.

Tanaquil had said, "You're thinking how I repaired the unicorn gate." And Tanaquil puzzled a moment then over what she remembered telling Lizra, at that time, about the gate, about the world beyond. It seemed to Tanaquil she had said very little, if anything at all, of the perfect world. Yet Lizra knew. As if she had read her mind. Tanaquil added, "But this isn't the same."

"I know you're brilliant," said Lizra, and flashed a false, charming smile, the sort she probably kept to win round bullish old counselors or obstreperous enemy commanders.

"Thank you," said Tanaquil.

She thought, I've come all this way, traveled all these miles, seen huge trees and talking statues, distant lakes and mountains— to come back and do this. To mend something.

But it was worse than that.

Lizra had had the unicorn made as the symbol of her power. The symbol of her mission to conquer—everyone, everything. And it had not worked. But now here was clever Tanaquil to make it go.

I've come all the way to glorify and help war.

Tanaquil felt sick.

When they had come out into the sunlight from the lamplit tent of the unicorn-machine, some men came hurrying up, and these were only halted by Lizra's soldiers with crossed spears. These men all wore black and red, and the buckles of their belts were shaped like hammers crossed by chisels. The badge of the Artisans Guild, Tanaquil recalled with displeasure.

The men bowed low.

"Empress," said the biggest man, who, thank the God, was not Vush (she would never forget the trouble she had had with Vush). "We heard you wished to see the unicorn. I should have been informed. Most remiss."

"Why?" said Lizra, coldly. Oh, so cold. Just like her father.

"But, Majesty—we *made* the unicorn—"

"So you did. Made something that doesn't work."

"An error, Greatness. We grovel. Only a short while and we will—"

"There's no need for that," said Lizra. "This lady is a competent sorceress and will fix everything."

The artisans scowled.

Tanaquil thought, Lady, but not "sister." Sorceress, too. Lizra had made magic legal and acceptable, providing it was also of use.

The biggest artisan, who had a silly little pink moustache, spread his arms. "These things should be left to the guild, Luminous Madam."

"I am the law," said Lizra. "The guilds are my servants."

That was all.

The artisans folded into bows and were very quiet as Lizra and Tanaquil walked away between the tents, and the soldiers started up again like clockwork, cheering and applauding.

"Won't you have offended them?" asked Tanaquil.

"They have offended *me*."

Tanaquil thought, And one must never do that, obviously.

Around a curve of wagons and carts, where horses were being led to and fro, was another little camp. Every tent pitched here was of cloth-of-gold, although they were small as beehives. Women and men were cooking at fires, as elsewhere through the main camp, but seeing Lizra's silver figure, they all stood to attention, letting the food burn. Some others crawled out of the tents. They kissed the ground, and Tanaquil heard the old cry she recollected: *"Lizra! Lizra!"*

Lizra said, fondly, "These are the stokers. They belong to the unicorn. I let them use my pet name."

A skinny man in an orange shirt came over and got down and kissed the ground.

"Princess-Empress!"

"Good evening, Bump. I've good news. Soon the unicorn will be working."

"Oh, Madam," said Bump, gazing at Lizra with adoration.

"Then your job begins," said Lizra.

"We run to it and fire it," cried Bump joyfully, "we pour in the water. The heat scalds, but who cares! We're your demons, Lady."

"Thank you, Bump."

Bump kissed the ground again.

A woman lifted up her baby and said loudly to it, "Look, there's the Empress. You'll be able to boast you saw her, when you're grown up."

"There is an ant," said Tanaquil to Bump, "trying to go up your nose." Bump brushed at his face. "You should be careful of ants," said Tanaquil. "They defend their queen. They fight for her and go to war. They carry things. They name all their children after her."

Bump only beamed.

Tanaquil realized she was not being fair. Bump had to be civil to Lizra. There he was, kissing the ground again as they walked on.

When they got back to the huge gold tent, Honj and his men had ridden off somewhere. A momentary look of disappointment went over Lizra's face. Then she was gracious again. She let Tanaquil into the tent and took her directly to her own empressly apartment.

Five servants began to spread out sumptuous dresses, so Tanaquil could choose her attire for tonight's feast. She and Lizra were still the same size.

"I'd rather just wear what I have."

"Oh. That brown thing. No, choose something elegant."

"Don't you remember," said Tanaquil, "how the peeve and I spoiled your dresses before?"

"I have a thousand gowns with me, or is it a thousand and ten?" said Lizra casually. "And the conquered cities are always making me more. Last week one arrived sewn all over with fireflies."

"How cruel," said Tanaquil.

"Oh," said Lizra, "they'd killed them first."

"That's all right then."

In one of the tent rooms they had, in crystal cups, juice made of quince and pineapple, white wine, and buns on plates of gold.

"I know I'm being a bad hostess," said Lizra, "but, Tanaquil, could I ask you to work on the unicorn tonight? After dinner, of course. It's an early start in the morning, you see, and my scouts have reported the town may have sent an army against me, again. It will be a pitiful force, probably, but people can be so stupid. They won't just give in. I always say, if a town or city surrenders, they'll be treated with honor. But half the time they don't, and we can't."

"You can't treat them with honor."

"No. Obviously, we have to make an example."

"Yes."

"I hate it. Burning their houses and—and the other things. The unicorn could stop all that."

"It will frighten them so much," said Tanaquil. "No one will resist."

"*Yes.* That's it."

"Whose idea was it?" Tanaquil said suddenly. "The unicorn. Was it your—was it Prince Honj?"

"No. It was my idea. I never forgot the unicorn of the city. I've always thought that it came—not for my father—but for me. To bring me greatness."

"It only wanted to go back through the gate."

But Lizra was not listening.

Now Tanaquil, alone in her own room with the borrowed dress—a thing of white silk and blue beads—at least it was not pale green—thought about Lizora Veriam's unicorn of war. And thought about Lizora Veriam.

Lizra had grown up as Zorander's daughter. That was enough in itself. And then her friends—the envious, resentful girls of the alleys, the road-sweeper's daughter who had tried to cut Lizra's throat, but—"Poor Yilli was my mistake," Lizra had said. She held Yilli out of a window, let her escape. Lizra now would probably have let Yilli fall. Or would she? *Would* she?

The friends, anyway, had culminated in Prince Honj.

Tanaquil thought, And suppose I can't mend the unicorn, can't make it go?

What then? Would Lizra lose interest?

She remembered too how Lizra had said goodbye before, pressing jewels on her, concerned only with her shocked father, and looking already like a queen.

There was a noise outside. Shouts, horses, laughter. The Locusts had come back and were up to something. They were "great jokers."

Tanaquil frowned.

I'm jealous, she thought. Would I have liked my sister better if I'd finally had her to myself?

The peeve, which had been asleep in the empress room, woke up for the feast.

There was no serious talk, as tomorrow the serious business of conquest would be resumed.

Honj, sitting at Lizra's right hand, gave a brief lecture on desert animals, particularly peeves.

The table was long, and draped with white damask embroidered by large red and blue roses. The plates were of the usual gold, and the silver goblets had jewels set in them. Sometimes a guest would be invited to keep a goblet. He or she would then charm and carry on as if they had been invited into Heaven. There were no other pets.

People petted the peeve, which seemed intent on continuing its act of sickening furry adorableness that Lady Mallow had so loved. It sidled up to captains' ladies, and chirruped at them, ogling their food with popping yellow eyes until they fed it.

"One of the most intelligent animals of the desert," said Honj. "For example, they even seem to talk."

Tanaquil tried to disguise her anger. Honj, obviously, had been let in on the secret of the peeve's magically acquired, and frequently unfortunate, knack of speech.

"Peeve," said Honj, and the peeve looked at him, slightly less adorable, and more wary. "Catch!" said Honj, and threw a slice of gravied meat, splashing several people as he did so.

The peeve caught the meat, which trailed from its jaws a moment like a brown beard, and then vanished.

"What do you say?" said Honj. "Was it good?"

"Good," said the peeve. "More?"

One or two of the guests exclaimed.

"It's just a bark," said Honj, airily. "It merely sounds like something you expect to hear. Ask Lady Tanaquil, the proud owner."

Tanaquil said, "Naturally, the Prince explains far better than I *ever* could."

Honj looked as if he were considering throwing a slice of meat in her face too. He did not.

"Now," said Honj, "perhaps the peeve would like to try some of this?"

The peeve, wary but willing, pattered directly over the table, upsetting a salt cellar and somebody's wine with its tail. Honj laid bare his plate, and the peeve, muttering, "Good, yes, eat, eat," buried its snout in the highly spiced food. After a moment it raised its head, nose wrinkled and eyes shut.

Honj snatched the velvet cap from his neighbor's head and caught the peeve's raucous sneeze in it.

Everyone laughed, except the neighbor, a commander of several years' standing, and the peeve—who, having blessed itself, resumed eating Honj's dinner. Honj drew another empty plate toward him, loaded it, and went on with his meal.

The commander was irritatedly shaking out his hat on the floor.

Not long after, a bell was struck by a servant, as on the previous night. It was midnight. A silence fell.

Lizora Veriam rose to her feet in her fringed gown of crimson and purple.

"Midnight. The Sacred Beast," she said.

The other guests had got up and they joined her in the toast.

Tanaquil angrily did so too, as she had the night before.

(And, to her extra anger, Honj winked at her over his cup.)

It was the old toast of Sea City. The toast to the unicorn.

She had told Lizra. She had *told* her. Enough, surely enough. The unicorn was not theirs. It was the creature of the perfect world.

And now this.

As they sat again, Lizra said to her softly, privately, "It's so kind of you, Tanaquil, to go and see to it tonight. You must be tired. But I'm so grateful."

Then Lizra told everyone to keep their goblets *and* their plates. Including the peeve.

She got up, and Honj walked after her, as he had yesterday, as he always, apparently, did. Through the dining room and out. Through the tent. Into her golden bedroom of the thousand and ten dresses, and the bed shaped like a star.

I can say I tried. And nothing would work.

Tanaquil had been conducted by four servants with torches and four soldiers with swords to the black tent of the monstrous machinery.

The peeve had come halfway. Then, scenting the night at last, it ran off with a mumbled "Do dung."

They bowed and saluted as they let her into the tent, and two of the servants rushed about to light the lamps.

The monster stood as it had before, save now a flight of steps led up its side, and on top of these a platform rested, under an opened panel. Cogs, clockworks gleamed there, and darkness held like compressed night as the lamps came up.

On the platform were fine tools Tanaquil did not need, for she had her own. Also a velvet chair with a cushion, and a tray of tasty snacks, a teapot, wine, even a meat bone—presumably for the peeve.

The servants bowed out. The soldiers stood to attention outside the tent. Nothing could get in. No one could get out.

Tanaquil had said to Lizra that afternoon, "Suppose I don't think I'm able. Suppose I don't really think I should—"

And Lizra, who was Lizora Veriam, had said, gently, "Well, Tanaquil. But I can't let you leave me. We've been parted such a long while. I couldn't let you go."

In other words, *You too are my prisoner.*

In other words, *Mend my unicorn, my thing of power. Do it, or—*

Or what?

Tanaquil looked up at the golden slope of the beast. But she saw only the night caught among its cogs. She saw only the darkness.

VI

It was black as night, black as every night of the world together, and it shone as the night shines with a comet. Mane and flaunting tail—golden-silver fire off the sea. Bearded in this fire, fetlocks . . . its eyes were red . . . it rose up to a height that was more than the room could hold—

Yes, that had been the unicorn. The being that came from, and returned to, the perfect world.

My unicorn—

No, not hers. Not Tanaquil's. But yet—the unicorn she had assisted. The unicorn that had touched her and perhaps worked great magic on her.

Not *this*.

It had magnificence, she could see that. Glamour and great strength. It stood there like a tower of golden coins.

The eyes were red glass, Lizra had said, many layers of it. They would burn up when it was heated through inside. It would, once it would work, stride forward, kicking its feet, terrifying the enemy, crushing them.

Tanaquil went down the platform and across the tent, her back to the golden monstrosity.

She opened the tent flap and looked out.

The guarding, imprisoning soldiers were all there, wide awake and still as metal men—like the unicorn they protected.

What would they do if she simply walked away? Probably not much. A courteous hand on her elbow, *Allow me to guide you, Madam.* And then either back in the tent or straight to the Empress.

The camp lay mostly quiet under a moonless, cloudy sky some-times dotted by lost stars. Fires winked back at the stars. Horses snuffled and men snored sadly.

Over there the tiny gold tents of Lizra's stokers, dark and silent. And there, across the camp, the vast golden bulb of Lizra's tent, still lit up like a beacon. Where Lizra lay beside her handsome lover, Honj.

The camel had been stabled near to the Empress's chariot horses. Old and patient, it had not objected, although the horses had made a fuss.

Could Tanaquil reach the camel somehow? And then, would the protection her own—it had, for a moment, been hers—her own unicorn placed on her cover her against assault?

Tanaquil sighed.

Or she could just go back to the golden unicorn and mess it up properly. Make sure it never *would* go.

Jaive had told her she too was a sorceress. It was well known that what a sorceress did well she was unable to do badly. And Tanaquil—mended, put right.

She thought of the stars of the perfect world, which had formed pictures all over the nighttime sky—kings and snakes and maidens.

For an instant, her eyes filled with tears.

She shook herself. *Don't be a fool.*

Something was running up through the camp, diving through stacks of gear and the embers of fires, causing little outbursts of curses and shouting. The peeve.

"Huge night!" it cried, running up to her in a glow of enjoy-ment. "Saw beetle like button. Pretty. Foxes—chased. *Hill.*" It turned and looked into the tent. "What there?"

"Come and see."

The peeve waddled into the unicorn tent.

It looked up at the unicorn. For about three seconds. Then it sat down and scratched vigorously. Having done that, it looked up again, but this time at the platform. It scuttled over the steps, its tail slapping, and drank the cup of tea Tanaquil had poured. Then it sat down to the meat bone.

"Bone!"

"Yes. Don't you think you've had enough?"

"Appetite," said the peeve, which sometimes now produced quite large words.

"And what do you think of that?"

"Bone."

"No, I mean the golden thing."

"What thing?" said the peeve. It lost attention and began to crack the bone for the marrow.

For the peeve, the golden unicorn did not count.

Tanaquil walked up the steps and looked in at the panel. Perhaps the peeve was right.

She put her hands in among the wheels and levers and gears. It felt flat and dead. Perhaps she *would* never be able to repair it.

Then she sensed the wrongness. Something was missing. They had left something out.

She drew back.

The peeve was sitting in a dish of cake, chomping the bone, and otherwise a vast quietness lay on everything. The matter was settled. Some vital piece had been left out of the machine and she did not know what it was. Tanaquil sat in the velvet chair. She need do nothing more.

Tanaquil raged. Prince Honj the mercenary was riding a black unicorn over the flowery plain. But unicorns were not horses—you did not ride them—in the perfect world even horses were not ridden—

She shouted, but her voice cracked. He had not heard, or if he had, did not care. Besides, the unicorn *allowed* it.

The peeve pulled at the white earring in Tanaquil's left ear. "Snail," it announced.

But the earrings, both of them, were not snails. They had been the ultimate keys to the unicorn gate, and when she had dismantled it, she had had them made into jewelry so that she would never lose them and they could never again be put to use.

The peeve pulled on the earring, hurting her ear.

"Stop it," she yelled at the peeve, and "Stop it!" she yelled at Honj.

"Yurrp," said the peeve.

It lay warm and weighty with cake and bone on her lap. It had not been pulling her earring. She had fallen asleep in the velvet chair.

The walls of the tent were a paler black, and through the flap showed a thin crease of gray. Daylight was coming, and already the noises of the camp were different. They were preparing to move, to march on another town.

Tanaquil put her hand to the left earring and took it off. She looked at it. A creamy whorl, a fossil.

She thought, if she had been able to push the center up, and uncoil the fossil, the spiral shape would have straightened into the exact image of a unicorn's horn.

And then she knew. She knew what was missing from the unicorn of gold.

"No," Tanaquil said, "I won't."

"Yurrupy," said the peeve, turning round on her lap to get more comfortable.

Tanaquil sat stunned, burning. She mended. That was her sorcery. And here she had the key to the mending of the machine that would not go—and she wanted to forget that. She wanted to say to Lizora Veriam, Sorry, I couldn't.

But magic did not work like that. It was as if she must—

It came to her that perhaps magic had gone into the mechanical unicorn too, and that this compelled her.

Already she was lifting off the protesting peeve, and standing up and walking to the open panel in the unicorn's side.

It gleamed only dully now that the lamps were out, and before the sun had come. Like old honey that had thickened in the jar.

She slid her hand forward, and something pulled on her and on the white fossil key, just as the peeve had done in the dream. The fossil was thrust, dragged into its place.

Tanaquil snatched back her hand. She looked around in a sort of madness.

There was no fire in the unicorn at least; there were coals, but unlit, and water, but it was cold in the pipes. Nothing could happen. But then—what had Lizra said—every morning the stokers came, or one of them, and dropped in the fire to the brazier in the unicorn's belly. The fires always went out. And the stokers went away and someone told Lizra.

The army was on the move. She could hear it. The stokers would not come this morning.

In the tent wall the gray crease widened, and someone hurried bustling in.

It was a small, skinny man in orange. The stoker called Bump. He saw Tanaquil at once and bowed almost double, so for a ghastly moment she thought he was going to kiss the ground to her too.

"Morning, Lady. Sorry to interrupt. I have to set light to the coals, you see. Do it every day, like. Don't expect it's ready yet—"

"No," said Tanaquil numbly.

"Never mind. Have to do it. Ritual and that."

He came merrily up the steps and paused to pat the unicorn on the side.

"Marvelous thing. A real wonder of the world. And once you get it going, there'll be no holding us."

"No."

As merry Bump trotted past her, she slammed shut the panel in the unicorn's golden side.

She watched him scramble up on the unicorn's back. He said, happily, "Usually have to climb a leg to do this." He lifted some hatch above the tail, peered down, then took a wad of material from his belt, struck flame, and lit it. "Here we go," said Bump. "Soon have you up and off," he added to the beast. And dropped in the flaming wad.

Tanaquil stepped back. She did not know what she anticipated. Nothing happened.

Bump was scrambling down, using after all the golden airy strands of the tail, the left back leg, landing agile as a fly on the floor.

"Good morning, Lady."

And he was gone.

The peeve, which was finishing the cake, flailed when Tanaquil picked it up. But she got it down the steps, and they stood together on the ground, the peeve lashing its tail.

"Want eat," said the peeve.

"Not there."

The peeve considered. It lifted its face and its ears went up.

"Clocks," said the peeve.

Tanaquil could hear nothing, but she guessed the peeve's acute ears had picked up some sound from the mechanical unicorn. Was it only the fire in the brazier going out?

The peeve flattened itself to the ground. It snarled.

And then Tanaquil heard the ticking after all, loud and hard, like small blows struck on the inside of the metal. There was a smell too, faint and oily and tart, that she had taken for the after-odor of the tinderbox. But it was growing stronger.

Maybe these things always occurred, the brief effects of the lighted wad going down.

Then a soft, shrill creaking came from somewhere up in the air. It was like a complaining cry. Something stiff and unwilling and malign had been forced to move.

Tanaquil was dizzy—no, it was not that at all. It was—it was the golden ray of the horn. The horn was spinning slowly, its spirals seeming to bore through the air and away and away forever—

The groan of angry metal came again.

The left forehoof of the unicorn rose. And dropped back suddenly.

"Peeve, come here. I must warn them—"

Tanaquil, hauling the snarling peeve, got to the opening of the tent and burst out.

The soldiers turned and seemed to block her way.

"It's started—" she cried. "Move away! You must move back! And *they* must be told."

The soldiers looked at each other. They seemed less certain, less unreal. One said, "The unicorn—she's got it going."

Then there came a high, unearthly scream from inside the black tent, and there was a rush of hot, wet wind that smacked out against them.

The soldiers scattered aside. But the camp, in the turmoil of departure, did not hear or see.

Tanaquil thought, They don't know what they've done. They

don't understand it. She gave the nearest soldier a push. "Sound an alarm."

"Can't, Madam. That's only for when we sight the enemy." His idiocy was prompt.

Behind them, another shudder of heat went over the tent, and now there was a rising noise, terrible in its absurdity. It was as if a giant pan of stew was boiling over.

Tanaquil rapped the peeve on the rump. "Run!" It did as she said, sprinting off at high speed, between the legs of passing horses. Tanaquil shouted as loudly as she could: "The *unicorn*! The *unicorn*!"

Helmed heads turned, and there were now excited exclamations. Men pointed at the tent, which was pulsing with a full fiery glow.

The sun had just come up. It was dull also, the gray-red color the tent was going. The sky was overcast and dark.

The whole picture became ominous and fearful in this unhopeful light. The lines of men and horses, the great somber banners with their golden unicorns, the polished cannon on their carts. Only some extra horror seemed needed. And it was coming.

There was a terrific bang.

Horses neighed and reared, men howled and swore, things dropped. A shaft of blood-red sun came from the wrong side of the sky, out of the black tent, which abruptly blew upward and crumpled down, like a broken wing.

It stood above them. It was their symbol and the mark of their power and their right. But it was not their friend. No one's.

Bloody gold, it boiled. Steams were hissing from its every joint, and its hoofs were wreathed in steam as if it stood on clouds.

As the tent fell away, the unicorn tossed its head. It was an awful motion, not animal, but that of some dreadful doll. And then from its nostrils two bright gusts of flame shot out.

The army cheered. And the cheer sank off into a wavering uncertainty.

For now the golden unicorn came prancing forward, and as it came, it kicked, and three men rolled away shrieking.

Heat blasted from it. Its red eyes glared.

Its mindless head went up and down and its horn bored into the sky.

The army broke and ran.

Tanaquil went with it.

Behind her she heard tents falling and snapping as they were scorched and trodden flat. She heard the squealing of panicking horses and the roars of men and the high crying of women. Explosions came as the beast crushed through the fires.

Its direction was straight forward, thoughtless, reasonless, and unstoppable. It passed by the golden tents of the stokers, who ran out yelping, and by the golden pavilion of the Empress it passed like a blazing gale.

Lizra had come out, and she looked. Her face, even over all the distance, Tanaquil saw was flushed with joy and pride. The only beautiful thing to be seen.

VII

"Only nine men died, Empress. And twenty-three were hurt. They're honored. And the dead—pleased to give their lives for the glory of Sea City."

Lizra nodded.

Tanaquil thought, Does she really believe that?

The unicorn had gone on, over the plain, into some low hills. It scorched its way with a path of burning. Its path was easy to follow: brown and black, the green grass and the flowers. *Like the path of withering I made in the perfect world.* Tanaquil had shut her eyes.

When the fuel was consumed, water and coals used up, steam exhausted, the unicorn stopped. Gradually, it cooled. Rabbits were playing nearby when the soldiers found it.

Then they brought it back on a sort of sled. Servants flew to grease the runners. It careered down into the camp, where the other three sections of the army were riding in.

Although nine men had died, the unicorn was cheered. It was theirs.

"The Lady Tanaquil," said Lizra, to her captains and commanders, "did this. She is a great sorceress. My companion."

Companion, not sister.

Honj laughed. Tanaquil saw him.

And later Lizra said to her: "They've brought your camel, Tanaquil. I should ride with the women, if I were you."

The campaign was so certain that the captains had all brought their wives and lady friends. There were the wives of the soldiers too. Tanaquil rode her camel, then, among their carts and carriages. The peeve sat bolt upright, staring about.

I've done what she wanted. I could escape now.

But the spell of the unicorn was on her. She had been linked to its foul, evil stupidity. She was to blame. The unicorn and Lizra's changed personality and the mockery of Honj—these things tied her to the army and to the war like chains of iron.

When Lizra's army had all joined up, it was thousands strong. Tanaquil never accurately found out how many. But it seemed to stretch for miles, a dark mass of men and horses and equipment, cut by the flare of banners and the flash of swords.

They reached the valley below the town (Ulp and Mallow's town) about sunset.

The Empress ordered a halt. They would attack by night.

There was a dinner in the golden pavilion, which had been set up again in the valley, by a picturesque stream. And Lizra, seeing Tanaquil in the blue and white dress, said, quickly, softly, "Oh, Tanaquil. You must always send for a new gown. Something new every night." That was all. A little warning.

She wants me to stay too. In case I can do anything magical and useful. But I must be properly dressed.

Honj swaggered in in a gorgeous garment of black and gold. His hair, dark brown with rivers of blackness in it, caught the lamps and shone nearly red, as the overcast sun had done, going down.

He fed the peeve and then sat at table grooming it with a stiff brush. The peeve became impossible, rolling about and growling with delight. Sometimes it would help, bringing up a back leg: "Flea *there*."

This was a business dinner, however.

After only an hour of eating, plates were cleared and Lizra stood up.

"Perhaps there won't be any siege. We have our figurehead now, our unicorn."

She described the attack—this battalion going here, and that one there, the unicorn marching before them all.

The accidents of the morning had taught a lesson. The unicorn needed to be pointed in the proper direction, which in this case was the town gates.

"I will of course," said Lizra, "ride behind the unicorn in my chariot. The Prince will be, as ever, my guard."

The peeve followed Honj out into the firelit night.

Tanaquil stood beside the stream.

The camp was very noisy, eager. Lights shone and flamed on all sides, growing tiny in the distance as the fireflies sewn on Lizra's dress. Somewhere, aloof, a nightingale sang.

Honj was playing with the peeve on the stream bank, throwing sticks, which the peeve caught, teaching it new words: "Muttok," "cookery," "aubergine."

"Ah, haughty Lady Tanaquil," said Honj. "Will she change me into a stone?"

"Did you want very much to be one?" asked Tanaquil.

"Oddly enough, and much to your disgust, I like what I am. I like being myself."

"I'm sorry."

Honj laughed.

"As if you cared, Madam. I tell you now, I was born in the slums and grew up in poverty. Where I am now suits me better."

"And where are you?" Tanaquil asked bleakly.

"On the winning side."

"On Lizra's side."

"There are worse places. She's been good to me."

"I'm glad," said Tanaquil, "you've noticed."

Honj threw a stick and the peeve leaped. The afterglow, the lamps, the fires, all touched its eyes, and his.

"You're too hard on me."

Tanaquil said to the peeve, "Come here, now."

The peeve, crestfallen, came to her.

"Loyal," said Honj.

"Oh," said Tanaquil, "you know that word too, do you?"

"We move on the town in two hours," he said. "Where will you be?"

"Safe. She's told me to stay with the women."

"How curious, when you are a woman."

"So is she."

"No," he said, "*she* is the Empress."

The nightingale stopped singing.

There was a sound of feet pounding up the bank. Someone splashed through the stream and then, nasty in the vague light, there stood the Locust Mukk.

"Honj, they've caught a spy from the town."

He was a little man, the spy, and he had admitted at once what he was up to. He had not wanted to come, but one of the lords in the town had bullied and paid him. He had known he would get caught, and so he was.

"There's an army going to march out," said the spy, somewhere between boasting and embarrassment.

"A very large army?" inquired Honj.

"Oh, go on," said the spy. "I can't betray my own town."

"Let's heat up the pincers," said Turnip, "eh, Honj? Warm him up a bit."

The spy quivered. Honj only said, "We know about your army. At the most it's six hundred strong. Do you begin to guess how many men the Empress has here?"

"A lot," said the spy.

"I think you'd better go back," said Honj. "Find the lord who sent you and tell him to tell your town that they haven't a hope. I'll give them until midnight. Then we start."

"I'll never get there in time."

"Find him a fast horse, someone."

The spy was upset. He saw great matters resting on his shoulders.

"I'll tell you now it's all fighting talk down there," he said.

"They're mad," said Honj. "For God's sake, you've seen. You must put them off. The Empress will harm no one, if the town surrenders."

"We spit on your Empress," said the spy. He looked nervous. "No offense." The horse was brought, and the spy got up on its back after the third attempt. He sat there like a scarecrow. "We've been miserable for weeks," he confided to Honj. "We don't want to fight. We'll lose. We'll get hurt. But why does she want to come here and mess everything up? We were all right. I had a nice grocery business, milk fresh from the goat, nice cheese, a few cabbages. And now what? I could be dead by sunrise."

"Not if you surrender."

"Why should we?" demanded the spy. "Let your lot run all over us. We don't want you. Tell your Empress to go away. Go and marry someone and have a family. That'll take her mind off all this conquest nonsense."

"I'm afraid it wouldn't," said Honj. "And you've said enough. Get going before I let Turnip here practice his knots on you."

The spy galloped off.

Honj shrugged.

Tanaquil, who had watched from the shadows, said, "So you're merciful too."

"I'm lovely," said Honj. "You'd be surprised."

"Muttok," said the peeve, discarding a piece of leather it had been trying to eat.

"That's a foreign swear word," said Honj. "I won't tell you what it means."

Tanaquil rode the camel up the hill in the starlight. All around and below, the army of Empress Veriam was slowly moving, forming into its battle lines. In the dark it looked as if the earth itself were heaving, thrusting up men and machines. Torches flamed. The unicorns of the standards, the weapons, glittered.

And farther off, about a mile away, Tanaquil could now make out the white-walled town, with its roofs and towers and orchard trees. And on the plain beneath, another moving mass sprinkled by lights, that was the town army.

At least Ulp and Mallow were away in their villa. At least, when the battle and the siege were over, Tanaquil would not have to be afraid of seeing their faces, among the frightened and furious faces of survivors or captives.

I could just ride off into the night. I know my mother is safe now, her land is Lizra's, the only place not due to be conquered.

But then, if Lizra meant to conquer the world, it would be impossible to outrun her.

The peeve scratched vigorously. "Aubergine," it said, with an air of being outrageous.

Then, far ahead, Tanaquil heard the wild cheering and clacking of shields start up.

Lizra was going through the army in her chariot, her black horses in their red war plumes, and herself clad in gold armor. Honj and his men rode at her back. And something else: Something else that shone.

It was big enough that she could see it easily, like an arch of gold: the unicorn on its sled being pulled into position at the very front of everything, angled correctly, toward the town on the plain.

The cheers and clacks increased.

Below and around the men roared, and the women at the back stood on their carriage roofs to see.

She ought to applaud too. She had helped make it ready.

Tanaquil looked about. There was no way off the hill but down and forward, toward the plain.

A streamer of boys passed with torches, calling excitedly, "Unicorn! Unicorn!"

From here, Tanaquil could not make out all the details. But she knew they would, Lizra's stokers, be pouring in the water, the fuel, and lighting the coals.

She had to see. Why? Tanaquil did not know.

She propelled the camel forward.

People got out of its large, soft-footed way. They knew it, and who rode it, and now they cheered Tanaquil. These were not the cheers Lizra had heard, not inspiring.

They were making a sort of avenue for her, thinking, presumably, she was trying to get to the Empress, and that she must be allowed to. Tanaquil was their sorceress.

She could imagine it whispered in the town.

"The enemy, the Mad Empress, has a *witch*."

Some of Lizra's army were even shouting it at her, full of enthusiasm: "The sorceress! Look, it's the sorceress and there's her funny animal that talks!"

"Aubergine," said the peeve, and curled up, putting its tail over its nose.

Tanaquil did not reach Lizra. The press of soldiers was now too thick and too disciplined to let her through. But down the slope she saw the unicorn of gold beginning to glow, and then she heard the noise as it stamped on the sweet summer earth.

The whole army leaned forward. Even the banners pointed. Somewhere a note was struck—perfect timing.

"Midnight! The Sacred Beast!"

It was rumbled and squalled from so many thousand throats.

A blush of white steam went up into the air. The unicorn shifted. It took three paces. The army yowled with happiness.

And then the unicorn was striding ahead, shaking its feet. It was a colossus, and it *burned.* Light came through it, and out at every chink. It was a thing of fire. It lit up the night.

Even here, Tanaquil smelled its stink of acids and oils and tinders and hot metal.

Sparks showered up into the black sky.

Tanaquil imagined the nightingales of the plain all stopped at once, like clocks, night things rushing to their burrows. The flowers would crisp and scorch. She could smell that too, an aroma like toasted hay.

The army roiled after the unicorn that was its emblem, and after the gold Empress in her chariot.

Tanaquil was borne with it, the camel stepping gamely.

On the valley floor tiny bugles were blowing. A bell rang somewhere.

As the ranks of the army moved faster, Tanaquil found it easier to guide the camel between the horses. Battle-trained, they let it pass. The men looked faceless now, their features half concealed by helms and masks, blank as disks. They were hypnotized.

So at last, she got in among the force that rode behind Lizra, and saw Honj's men, upright too on their horses, blank and coin-faced like the rest, spears and swords drawn and glistening in metal-gloved hands. Honj she did not see. She wondered if he also had this look.

But what was she doing? She had never learned to fight hand to hand. She would not be able to defend herself—

The unicorn blazed before them like a torch that walked by itself. The stokers skedaddled behind, busy like insects, yipping to each other. Billows of steam and waves of heat must be scalding them. But they paid no attention. Now one darted forward and scrambled up a moving golden leg and poured in water at a spout. Surely the unicorn was too hot to touch? Tanaquil remembered the insane chair-gangs of Zorander's palace. She shuddered. And nearby a man muttered, *"Death or glory!"*

Probably the descent through the valley took twenty minutes. It seemed to go on and on forever, and also to be over in a minute.

All at once Tanaquil grasped that she could glimpse the opposing army bunched there, between them and the white, unstained walls of the town.

Now this opposing army was disintegrating. They were screaming and running away as the towering fire of the unicorn ploughed among them.

Huge black shadows smothered the white walls, cast away from the unicorn's advancing light; shadows of men running and screaming and falling down.

It had been exactly primed, the unicorn. It rolled on, stepping and kicking over men, and now it went through a line of peach trees, and it swung with its horn, and, oh, the delicious smell of cooking fruit, like jam—

When it hit the gates, it hit them like a battering ram on legs. It kicked.

Huge splinters flew into the sky like startled birds.

The gates of the town gave way.

The unicorn pushed through, and as it brushed the wall sides, fire sprang off from it.

There was a juddering sort of halt.

Some fighting had broken out. About thirty men from the town army had tried to attack the front line of soldiers about the Empress's chariot. Swords like silver needles flickered, sewing up holes of color and dark.

But the fighting was over in a moment, dealt with, and instead a great voice was beginning to swell up from the town itself. Smoke was lifting in heavy clouds, and a red reflection. The bell rang on and on, and with it now, not nightingales, but the thin whistling noise of wailing children and shrieking women. The unicorn, striding before them, had set the town alight. But then the town had not surrendered. They had had to be shown.

VIII

In the morning, after the fires had been put out, the town was not white anymore. Its towers were black with smoke. Roofs had burned off. The air was thick with cinders. Everything smelled . . . like the unicorn.

The unicorn itself stood in the fields beyond the town. Much of the corn had burned too, and so the golden beast waited in the middle of a black wasteland. The soldiers, some of them, were having a party around it. They had thrown garlands of flowers up over its horn and its arched neck. But they did that too soon, before it properly cooled, and the flowers had withered to shriveled brown papers.

It did not look either as it had. The unicorn, they said, had honorable battle scars. The internal heat had caused some of the gold plates to melt. In parts, the metal had bubbled. Here and there a stripe of iron was left bare. A black mark. As it had walked through the town, kicking things over, striking sparks against bells and chimneys, setting walls alight with its scalding, the glass eyes had got so hot that they burst away like drops of blood. The unicorn would need new eyes. The artisans were hurriedly seeing to it.

One of the unburned palaces in the town had been made Lizra's headquarters, and here she sat in a hall painted with charming scenes of green meadows. Her throne-chair had been brought in for her, and she was surrounded by admirers and captains.

The rich people of the town who were able to walk had also been brought. They stood in a group on the pretty marble floor, their clothes torn and dirty and reeking of soot, as if they had been dragged all night through chimneys. Some of them cried. Others were hollow-eyed and firm. Through the windows, views of the ruined town were visible, and noises came in of Lizra's soldiers looting the houses for valuables, and so on.

"You have only yourselves to blame," said Lizra.

No one agreed.

She held out her hand for a list, and read off the names of other nobles who had perished, and buildings that had been destroyed.

"I came here," said Lizra, calmly, "to make you happy. And now I shall do it. I shall restore order. I shall bring you into the union which I am creating."

"Give me back my son!" a woman shouted.

She was shushed uneasily.

Lizra said, "Your son should not have opposed me. Then you would still have him."

Presently, the lords and ladies were herded away to a room where they were offered the chance to sign a paper declaring Lizra Empress and Mother to the town.

Lizra and her commanders went outside, and Tanaquil, who had watched the scene in the hall, now watched a scene in a filthy courtyard full of broken things, where worried hens were running about.

To some posts had been tied up the few men who had foolishly resisted Lizra's army. Foremost among these were an elderly white-haired man and a dark-haired young man tied back to back.

Honj stepped forward, and Lizra asked him who this odd pair was. "The old one is too old to fight," she remarked. At which the old one laughed scornfully.

"Be quiet," said Honj, "I strongly advise you."

"Don't care," said the old man.

"Nor do I," said the young one.

"A grandfather and his grandson," said Honj. "It's interesting. The old one's son, who is the father of the young one, is even now assisting your soldiers in entering the houses."

The grandfather spat. The young one spat.

Lizra said, "I remember them both running at me with raised swords."

"Never thought," said the grandfather, "I'd lift my hand to a woman. But you're the devil, girl."

Lizra said, seriously, "I am the Empress." She indicated the burned town, the piles of debris, the frightened chickens. "I've come to bring order, peace, and happiness."

The grandson said, "You're a bitch."

Lizra said, "They must be made an example of. They must both be beaten, one hundred lashes, in the town square."

Honj looked at the grandfather and the grandson. Neither showed they had heard. Honj said, "Well, Madam. I think they're beneath you. Look." He stooped and picked up a small white egg that one of the hens had just deposited near his boots. "This is the town. And this—what you've done to it." He crushed the egg, and yolk and shell ran down on to the ground. "Need you do more?"

Lizra gazed at him. Even with yolk on his hand, Honj looked wonderful.

"All right," she said. "Very well. I've done enough."

Tanaquil thought, He's saved them. They were lucky.

She felt a little dizzy, and leaned on a wall.

A moment later, Lizra, in her golden armor, walked past Tanaquil—and recognized her, which Tanaquil had not thought she would. "Isn't it a lovely day?" said Lizra.

Tanaquil did not manage to answer. And Lizra walked on, with all her retinue clanking and scampering around her.

Tanaquil went over and dragged the peeve out of the raw egg, which it was eating. She fastened its leash, and pulled it, protesting, back into the palace. There she sat on a bench, and the peeve sat down philosophically at her feet to give itself an eggy wash.

Everywhere people were rushing importantly by, this way, that way. There was an air of business and work to be done, and self-congratulation.

Somewhere out in the town, a woman's shrill scream seared into the sky, and faded.

Then, under the windows, she heard a weird, low grumble. "Where's Bump? That's what I want to know. Where is he? Where's Bump?"

Bump, the stokers' leader, chief attendant to the unicorn. Probably out in the fields, tying daisy chains on its neck—

"Oh, what a sad sight," said a male voice closer to hand. "The sorceress lost in melancholy."

It was Honj.

He had come in at the door, and stood, scraping something off his boot with a stick.

"Why," said Tanaquil, "did you save that old man and the young one?"

"Why not?"

"That isn't a reply."

"Dear me. Whatever shall I do?"

Tanaquil said, "Did you feel sorry for them?"

"Partly. And for her."

"For *Lizra*?"

"Yes. She has terrible nightmares when she exacts punishments like that."

"Oh, I see. And it keeps you awake. Now I understand."

Honj grinned. He had two faultless rows of straight white teeth. "She told me to tell you that you must meet her in the Crystal Chamber at noon."

"Me? Why does she want me?"

"To discuss your future usefulness, I imagine."

"I'm not useful. I don't want to be useful. Not—for *this*."

"We all have qualms," he said. "At least you weren't sick. After my first battle I threw up. It was behind an inn. I'll never forget the bricks in that wall."

Tanaquil said, "But now you're quite happy about it all." She added, "And where is the Crystal Chamber?"

Honj pointed at the ceiling. "Upstairs. An old banquet room. Lizra was taken by it, so nothing got smashed."

The peeve went over to Honj. "Stick?"

"No, you wouldn't like this one. Wait till tonight. We'll have a proper game."

Tanaquil thought, Even the peeve has fallen for him. So much for loyalty.

"What's happened," she said, "to Bump?"

"Who's Bump?"

"One of the stokers."

"Oh . . . yes. Disappeared, I believe. No doubt in the alehouse."

Far off, streets away, something fell with an awful crash.

Honj swung out and was gone.

The light on the floor had moved. It would be noon in half an hour.

Tanaquil investigated and found a broad white stair, on which someone had left a saucepan. It looked so sad, it almost made her weep, and she drove her nails into her palms.

She climbed the stair as if she carried the town on her spine.

Lizra was late, of course. An Empress would have to be.

She came in clothed in a dress of fine-spun bright pale green— the proper wear of the young—and a coronet of emeralds.

"Oh, Tanaquil. Don't you like this room. I think I'll have this palace made over for my use, sometime, if ever I come back here."

Tanaquil peered around at the room. It had many windows, which, rather than looking out on the town, were full of silvery pictures in glass—beasts and lovers and trees of fruit. All the things, maybe, that had just been spoiled. From the ceiling hung lamps that were in turn hung by prisms. Everything sparkled. It meant nothing, and Tanaquil forgot at once what she had just been looking at, as had happened after she first came in.

"He said you wanted to see me."

"Who did? Oh, Honj. Must you be so coy? One day Honj will be my consort. He'll be a king."

"I'm sure he'll be ever so pleased."

Lizra went to a chair and sat down.

"I'm exhausted. I didn't sleep all night. Too much to do. Tanaquil, I wanted to talk to you now, because maybe there won't be many more chances, for a time. There are three cities, six or seven towns in front of us. Three cities and seven towns to conquer. We'll be very occupied."

"Yes."

"And so here we are. A moment to be together."

Lizra looked at Tanaquil with an earnest, intense stare, and for a second, Tanaquil caught sight of a younger sister saying, You *are* excited, aren't you? You are on my side?

A tiny breeze blew through a tiny crack in one of the windows. It made the prisms tinkle. It smelled of burning.

"After the three cities, Tanaquil, we'll reach the sea. The Far Sea."

"And then you'll be Empress of all these lands," said Tanaquil.

"And then I'll cross the sea, Tanaquil. Because I have to go on. The world is a big place. And meanwhile there is all the administration. Who's to stay behind and govern? Who's to go ahead as a messenger? These things matter."

"And you'll never," said Tanaquil, "be able to stop."

"One day. One day, it will all be done."

Tanaquil watched the peeve. It was hunting one of the crystal reflections over the floor, where the breeze had blown it.

Lizra said, "Tanaquil, do concentrate. This is about you."

"Me?"

"We shall have to cross the sea. I shall need many ships—and machines. Clever machines that cross water and are *better* than ships. Inventors have spoken of them. But it will take sorcery too. *True* sorcery. *Yours.*"

Tanaquil laughed.

Lizra clapped her hands. "You're pleased! Yes. That's so good."

"No. I'm appalled. I can't do anything like that."

"Tanaquil," Lizra was very serious, "you can do whatever you put your mind to. You're a great genius. Think what you've done—what you've *seen.* I always knew. Oh, if I'd had you with me from the beginning—flying machines—you could make those. Yes, ships that cross the sky. And, Tanaquil—I must tell you. It's a kind of mad, wonderful dream . . ." Lizra held out her hand, but Tanaquil did not go to her; she pretended that your sister held out her hand to you simply as a gesture, like waving. Lizra said, "I heard an old woman singing a lullaby to a baby in my camp. Do you know what she sang? 'Hush, baby, don't cry. Look at the man in the moon; you don't see him crying. *They don't cry up there.*'"

Tanaquil did not laugh now. She swallowed.

"It was a song."

"Yes, but perhaps . . . One day, Tanaquil, you could help make me a vessel that would go up through the stars. Up to the moon."

The peeve pounced on the rainbow light. And growled, for there was nothing there.

Lizra said, "But that's for then. We have to reach the sea first. The Artisans' Guild is already making trouble. About what type of figureheads they'll put on the ships. And now," said Lizra, "we must have a meal. And then I have so many things to deal with. Stay with me. Stay and watch. Then you can help me."

"Where's Bump?"

It was a mutter going round and round the painted hall. You heard it crop up like a sigh or a whine under and behind all the urgent chat of war.

The captains had come and been commended.

Then the servants came and got orders.

Then, one by one, all the people who coped with the procedure of subduing and controlling the town.

"There will have to be an egg ration, your Luminescence."

"What are we to do about the water supply? It has sausages in it."

"Where's Bump?"

"The corn may be lost. Should we organize reapers?"

"Should the palace on the hill be demolished? It's liable to fall down."

"Where's *Bump*?"

Finally someone, a small dark man of the stokers, covered in bandages, for of course they had all been burned and scalded attending to the unicorn, hobbled forward.

"Mighty Empress Lizra, Bump's disappeared. And so has Wijel."

Lizra, who had been answering, and conferring with counselors all afternoon, looked at the stoker.

"Disappeared? Explain to the Empress," boomed an adviser.

"Well, like, he was going up to see to the water, and he went."

"Went?"

"Vanished. And Wijel did too. But no one saw them go."

"Has Bump deserted?" asked the adviser.

"*Never!*" cried the stoker, and from the hall came hoarse cries of stokerish outrage.

Another one limped forward, sheepish, his hat in his bandaged hands. He kneeled and kissed the ground before Lizra's chair.

"Lady, he did what's unlucky. He ran under the unicorn. Never do that, we always say."

Tanaquil remembered how she and Lizra had walked under the unicorn's golden belly. It had *felt* unlucky. But the unicorn was a war machine. Lucky for some—

Somebody shouted at the back of the hall. A soldier came out, slightly drunk, so Tanaquil thought nostalgically of her mother's guard.

"Madam," said the soldier, "I have to report that Plip has vanished too. He walked under the unicorn in the field, to put a garland on it. And he went. And no one believed me. But where's Plip?"

"Where's Bump?"

Lizra said, "Then no one must walk under the unicorn."

She was tired. She looked like a brave little girl who has stayed up too long. She touched the arm of an adviser. "That's enough now."

Tanaquil watched Lizra walk out with her retinue. She realized, in relief, that Lizra had forgotten her again.

IX

Crows followed the army. They followed it through the world. And when the golden unicorn cooled, the crows would perch there.

It was not glamorous now.

It was horrible.

Like an old lava pool, all bubbled up, yellow and glittering, with long rents that showed black iron. Black unicorn under gold. Its eyes were always red, for the artisans replaced them after every battle, every skirmish, just as they hammered on new plates of gold. But the gold was always scabrous and uneven. Scars. It was a warrior.

And it was unlucky. More disappearances. Men around the unicorn vanished. They never came back. Others were scalded anyway, and laid up, left behind. New stokers. They had a battle cry: "The unicorn! Beware the horn! The kicking feet! The burning heat!" You could hear them feebly whispering this as they were carried off afterward.

The battles were large and small. Silly ambushes that were scorned at Lizora Veriam's feasts. Bigger things, where there were casualties, and the "enemy" was blamed.

And then no more battles. No more fights. The villages and towns surrendering, just as Lizora Veriam had told them they must. Crowds running out and throwing down flowers, the last of the year. Lizra, crowned by red roses, riding her chariot, so glad and happy, bringing joy and unity to the imperfect world.

And Tanaquil on the patient camel, with the peeve asleep, its sun-warm fur under her hand, her only comfort.

There was a great feast on a hillside; the second city had given in without a blow exchanged.

The city had made Lizra its Queen of Summer, some old title useful for the time. And Lizra had sat in a snow-white dress covered by gold, with red flowers in her hair again, and Honj was with her, also in white, and with a red rose on his collar.

Tanaquil watched them, her sister and her sister's lover, and at last Tanaquil knew, as if someone had slapped her face.

He is the reason I've stayed. I've hated it. I should have gone away. But he fascinates me too. The way he throws sticks for the peeve, like a boy. The way he rides by and is a man.

And Honj was Lizra's.

I am jealous of both of them, Tanaquil thought, biting her lip, rigid with rage, *of Honj taking my sister from me. Of helping her to become this monster that now she is. And of my sister, because she has Honj.*

I'll go in the morning.

No, I can't. We have to enter the city in a glorious progress. Afterward, then, when no one remembers I'm there.

Almost two months had passed. The summer was coming to its end. Outside the nightingales sang in the trees above a river.

I don't even like him.

Tomorrow. Or the next day . . .

"Are you all right?" asked Honj, appearing out of the shadows above the river.

"Thank you. Of course."

"I wouldn't stay here. The men are drunk and crazy. They might forget who you are."

"Everyone forgets who I am. Who am I? No one."

"Tanaquil," said Honj. "I thought you valued yourself."

"Why would you think that?"

"Why not?"

"I've been involved in this. Her war."

"And you hate her war."

"Obviously."

"Poor Lizra," he said. "She wants you to approve. She never had a mother. She never had a proper father. She's had to try to find both."

"You're saying you are her father and I'm her mother?" Tanaquil cackled bitterly.

Honj threw a stick for the peeve, which raced along the
bank, falling over frogs, which dashed into the water croaking
in affront.

"No. I don't know what I'm saying. I'm scum. What do you
expect?"

Tanaquil looked at him narrowly. No mockery had sounded in
his voice. He seemed solemn and still, and the rich red rose was
dying on his collar. He tore it off abruptly and dropped it in the
river. "Give the poor thing a drink."

"Poor Lizra. Poor rose. You're sorry for us all."

"Not for you," he said. "Oh, *not* you."

She was both glad and angry.

She said, "And did you have a father and mother, *Prince?*"

"Obviously. Both slapped and beat me. Later both abandoned
me. Imagine me at ten years old, left in a barn in the winter."

"How sad," snarled Tanaquil.

"It's true. And you?" he said politely.

"My mother is quite mad. I ran away from her."

The river sang, and the nightingales also, and over the slope,
some drunken soldiers.

"I must go back," he said.

"Good-bye."

The peeve came bounding with the stick and stopped in shock
at finding Honj no longer there. Tanaquil threw the stick. The
peeve loped after it, but not with the same exuberance. The night
had gone flat as old beer.

Soon Tanaquil walked up from the riverbank, up through the
trees, into the hilly land where, that night, the golden unicorn
stood, garlanded with flowers and crows.

They were flapping their wings and cawing sullenly, the birds,
as they settled to rest.

And shall I cross under the unicorn's belly?

The night was glowing-clear with stars and moon, and the
unicorn shone, and the hill shone too.

A few sentries stood around, drinking wine.

It had not been fair, what she had said about her mother, Jaive. But, after all, nothing was fair, was it?

Tanaquil thought of the perfect world, of the scent of night, *there,* and the tears ran down her face. Who was she? She had no idea. Why did she cry? For herself or for her world?

The peeve rolled in the grasses, seeing only the moon. But even the moon was not the same. Lizra wanted that too.

PART
Three

X

The fifth town was called Beehaif.

It lay at the foot of the hills, and deep forest stretched beyond it, blue and green, and copper where the summer was going out.

Ambassadors came from Beehaif in the late afternoon. They brought gifts and tokens of surrender. They were insistent that they surrendered. They said, urgently, to Lizra's officials, "Are you sure you've written it down? Are you? We *surrender*."

Some of the gifts were of a domestic nature, including two kettles of pure gold. There were also silver trays of food, cakes, and pickles and slabs of melting butter. And, in the middle, a complement: a golden unicorn two feet high, made entirely of cheese. It had red candied cherries for eyes.

They knew all about the unicorn.

They said they understood that it would be pulled through the town on a sled so that everyone could see it.

"Or we can start it up. Fire it," said one of the captains jollily.

The ambassadors from Beehaif turned pale. "No, no."

They gazed at Lizra and hastily told her that the whole town had been painted in her colors, blue and red, to honor her.

Lizra thanked them. She was always very gracious when the towns and cities gave in.

They asked about the unicorn again. They were obviously nervous, and so Honj and the Locusts took them to see it, where it stood on the hilltop, gleaming in the sunset.

It looked so awful now, so terrifying, that two of the ambassadors ran away. The soldiers laughed at them. They liked the unicorn and some of them called it by a pet name, *Sunshine*.

Sunset ran over Sunshine like blood. Sunshine's crimson eyes glowed. Roses and hyacinths were around its neck. It was scarred, deformed, the tall gold arch of its stomach—under which no one ever crossed—casting a deep shadow on the grass.

After the ambassadors had gone, everyone was up most of the night, preparing for another glorious progress in the morning.

Lizra's chariot horses were reshod, their plumes combed. She had decided to dress in a red gown, not in armor. Honj had selected a hat with a long bill. The Locusts washed their horses, and the rest of the men were burnishing weapons and putting flowers on the cannon.

Tanaquil walked slowly up and down the camp, looking at all this.

When the sun went, a cold wind blew over the hill.

They would winter by the sea, and there the artisans would make ships and Tanaquil would work magic on them. It was all planned.

Tanaquil had lost her chance to get away, for Lizra had begun to have her watched. There was always some strong man a few yards behind her as she walked, there to protect her and uphold her dignity. The women who insistently brought her dresses and jewels for Lizra's feasts had beady, intent little eyes.

She should have left when she told herself she would, after the second city surrendered.

Why had she stayed? She knew why. Honj had sat laughing at the dinner, the torches flashing on the white bars of his teeth. He had been abandoned at ten. Though she had sneered at him, she had considered this. Honj was the reason she had remained. Not Lizra, however Tanaquil might tell herself that Lizra could change.

And there was nowhere to run; she had already decided that.

After all, when Lizra saw that Tanaquil could *not* magic ships into the air or over the ocean, Lizra would probably be glad to see the back of her, and Tanaquil could go then, because by then Tanaquil would be so sick of *herself* she would only want to be a hermit in the desert.

Tanaquil could see Sunshine gleaming on the hill. The soldiers were pouring wine over it. A lot of the army was drunk. But

then that would hardly matter. There would be no fighting in
the morning.

Shortly after sunrise, an autumn storm rose up from the forest.
The sky turned black. Lightning bit. Thunder rolled around and
around the earth like a great drum. The rain exploded from the
sky.

The peeve wiggled its way down the camel's leg, and the camel
allowed it, used to this event. The peeve swam in the fresh pud-
dles, splashing excitedly. It liked the rain, although ponds and
baths did not appeal to it. The camel closed its nostrils disdain-
fully and flicked its ears.

Tanaquil pulled on to her red head a large, floppy straw hat.
As she did so, she set swinging the remaining earring in her right
ear. She had been meaning to remove it for months, but had
not done so—like other things. It would increase her ragamuffin
appearance, of which Lizra tried so hard to cure her. Only last
night a dress had arrived for Tanaquil's entry into Beehaif—as
the sorceress of the army, during progresses, she was now supposed
to ride just behind Lizra's chariot. The dress was boned, indigo,
and sewn with pearls. Well, the hat would protect the dress.
Tanaquil looked back to where the women's part of the camp,
not wanted on the progress, was happily going about in the rain,
cooking and shouting, among the muddle of wagons and chariots,
chickens, goats, and children. A woman's place. Yet, too, a woman's place was at the head of her legions.

Soldiers were lifting hung-over faces to the cool torrent.

"Peeve, come up. We're off."

The ranks had begun to surge forward, and here came the
inevitable steward, who always found Tanaquil.

"Madam. You must go up ahead at once. The Empress's chariot
is on the move."

"Oh, dear, is it?"

Tanaquil smiled feebly. The steward, hung with gold chains,
was getting very wet indeed.

"That hat, Madam—" he began disapprovingly.

"Oh, thank you. I'm glad you like it."

Tanaquil tapped the camel as the peeve came floundering up its leg.

She rode forward a little way and fetched up among the Locusts, a position she had adopted since first told to stay forward.

"Here she is!" crowed Spedbo, jeeringly. "My, what a hat."

"Jealous?" asked Tanaquil.

Mukk said, "I wish I hadn't woken up this morning," leaned over his horse to the right, and was sick, fortunately out of sight.

"Can't hold his drink," confided Spedbo. "Hey, Mukk. How about a nice fried egg? Bit of roast beef? *Lovely* cream trifle?"

Mukk arose and glared. Spedbo pulled a face, leaned over to the left, and was also sick.

The peeve hissed, and began to dry itself, uselessly, on Tanaquil's pearly gown.

The Locusts, Tanaquil thought, reminded her of her mother's soldiers at the fortress. These mercenaries had generally been quite reasonable to her, and seemed only mildly superstitious of her "magic." Probably, Honj had trained them to accept sorceresses as they had empresses. Did she only like the Locusts because they were his?

Half an hour later, they were on the slope, and the going was difficult. The rain licked out vast mud slides. Horses slithered and sat down. The men had changed from worshiping the rain to cursing it, sneezing and growling as it went down the necks of their mail shirts.

Mukk and Spedbo, however, had brightened, and were exchanging jokes. Tanaquil did not understand half of them, but they made her laugh because Mukk and Spedbo laughed.

Or did she only laugh because Honj would have laughed?

Over her shoulder Tanaquil glimpsed a burly man in ornaments, riding with nasty little eyes only on her. Lizra's guard-watcher.

"What's up?" asked Mukk.

"That man is following me."

Mukk looked. He bellowed at the burly man, "You! Clear off. The Lady Tanaquil is with us."

"Orders of the Empress," said the burly man.

There, it was out.

"Am I under arrest?" asked Tanaquil.

"Your protection, Madam. Especially among these ruffians."

"Who are you calling a ruffian?" howled Spedbo. "What's it mean?" he added to Mukk.

But they were involved in Lizra's progress. A brawl was out of the question, for now.

It occurred to Tanaquil that the Locusts themselves might enable her to get away, at the proper moment.

Through the rain the town began to loom.

It looked—awful.

All its heights, its belfries, towers, and pinnacles, had been painted bright piercing blue, and elsewhere it was a surly red. The walls were a patchwork.

"They've done a lovely job," said Turnip, from in front.

He really thinks so!

Bells were ringing through the rain, and as they got closer, vague cries of welcome expanded. The mud was worse. Tanaquil had been splashed to the waist, and the peeve (which had got down again once, to investigate something) appeared like an animal partly made of fudge.

A horse slid three lines in front of them, knocking into another, which shied and neighed.

Farther ahead, between the shapes of riding men and the silver thongs of the rain, a golden glimmer. Was it Lizra's chariot, or the unicorn?

Then the ground leveled into the valley, and only the heights of the town were visible, above the entering army. And beyond, the forest, black as night with water.

Tanaquil began to hear a soft, desolate sound. It seemed to come from the town, where the bells and cheering had been.

Then Mukk burst out laughing.

"Just see," he said.

Tanaquil did not know what he was talking about. In the rain it was not easy to make out anything. The town itself seemed to be melting and running away—

And then she realized that it was. It was *running* in the rain. All the garish, fawning paint, swilling off, and down the gutters of Beehaif.

What would Lizra, in her pride and glory, think of that?

An omen, Jaive would surely have said.

They were passing in under the gate, which bled red and blue, dripping on them, so the soldiers cursed louder and the horses shied far worse.

It was not orderly, let alone regal, their entry into Beehaif.

The road was all mud and swirling with murky purple, as if tons of badly made cordial had been spilled.

The cheers were sad and defeated. The people on the balconies, waving and throwing flowers, had themselves wilted, and some had gone inside. One wet peony caught Mukk in the eye, but when he raised his hand in salute, the girl who had thrown it was being smacked by her mother. "You wicked, stupid child! You could have blinded him. And then they'd kill us all. They'd set that great unicorn thing on us. We'd die."

Mukk looked confused, and ate the peony. The peeve watched greedily, trampling the muddy rain well into Tanaquil's skirt.

At a turn in the road, Tanaquil did see her sister up ahead, and in front, the machine of war. It was at that instant that the sled, on which the unicorn was being drawn, tilted in the slime of paint and rain and mud, and the unicorn slewed sideways, scraping all the plaster from a tall and important-looking wall. Women wailed in terror.

Lizra's chariot had reined in.

The black horses stamped in their glitter and gold-shod hoofs and tossed their plumes.

Tanaquil could see Lizra too, gazing out at the open square, dotted with soaked officials and the governor of Beehaif. The unicorn looked ridiculous. One leg had come off the sled; it was at an angle. The stokers had already gathered to lift and straighten it, but it seemed capable of nothing except perhaps falling over.

The dripping governor crept forward and bowed low to Lizra, holding out a silver key on a wet cushion that symbolized possession of the town.

"This is a joysome day for us, your Magnificence," he sniveled. "The sun shines on us at your arrival."

Lizra was impervious. She had lost her sense of humor. Even the Locusts did not snigger. Not even Honj, on his gray horse.

"What a fiasco," Tanaquil said aloud.

No one heard her, or if they did, no one reproved her or agreed. Nothing.

Lizra was taking the key. She looked so small. Slim and pretty and good, washed in the rain where everyone else seemed stained and muddied by it.

"This is the beginning of a new age," said Lizra, in a ringing, girlish voice.

The governor said, pathetically, "Our town—we tried so hard—it's gone mauve."

This was true. On all the buildings the colors had mixed. A mauve town. Not the emblem at all of the Empress.

XI

After the wet and uncomfortable and rather boring feast the governor had arranged—most of the food had already been sent to Lizra's army—Lizra withdrew her troops to the better-drained height of the hill camp. About two hundred soldiers and their officers stayed in Beehaif, looking forlorn and blowing their noses.

The army spent the afternoon, as the skies cleared and turned soft with late sun, wringing out its plumes and banners, rust-proofing its swords, shields, cannons, and other items. The unicorn had been put before the camp, where—when seen from the town—it would glow like a golden sun at sunset. But it too was wet, and the stokers were crawling all over it, rubbing it with oily rags. Its scars of black iron must not rust.

Lizra had called her commanders to her tent, and Tanaquil had also been informed she should be there. The normal war conference took place. Lizra promised decorations and medals, although no one had had to be courageous, except about the rain. The keys and emblems of all the cities and towns were laid out on velvet on a table. In a corner stood the cheese unicorn. The men cut slices off, and drank wine.

Tanaquil kept the peeve on its leash. It was still thick with mud, some of which now and then it shook off over the expensive floor covering.

"Nothing but victory," said Lizra, who had changed into another red dress. "God is on our side."

The captains applauded.

Honj, Tanaquil noted, did not.

"And what is the matter, Prince Honj?" asked Lizra abruptly.

"I beg your pardon, Madam," said Honj, "I was thinking of pigs."

Lizra's brows rose. She looked cold, pure and, for a second, frightful. "Pigs?"

"I can't really explain my lapse, Empress. I saw some pigs in the town. They were much happier in all the mud than your soldiers."

Tanaquil tensed so hard that she pulled on the leash and the peeve rolled to her side.

Did Honj think he could play games with Lizra, make jokes, where none of the rest of them could? In private, maybe. But *here?*

"Wurrup," said the peeve.

Tanaquil relaxed her hold. The peeve darted to Lizra. It flung its muddy self at her gown and pawed the silk. It said, clearly, "Empress! Goddess!"

There was a little murmur.

Lizra looked down at the peeve and the light in her eyes altered from cold to warm.

"Oh no," she said.

Honj said, "Yes, Madam. What the animal *seems* to say is the answer. We are only mortals. In the rain, less than the pigs from the stye. But you—pristine."

"A goddess," said one of the captains.

A huge silence came from the tent.

Tanaquil thought, In the God's name, what now?

Mukk, who was standing respectfully behind Honj, said, "Hey, Honj. What's that funny sound?"

Tanaquil felt herself begin to hear, as if she had been partly deaf until now.

There was a strange, prolonged, high-pitched scream. It was like steam from a kettle. At the same time, there was a droning noise—

Honj strode past Mukk, opened the tent flap, and went out. Captains crowded after him.

Tanaquil noted that Lizra stayed where she was. Her face was so pale and locked in. She was thinking only of that wonderful word *goddess*. Tanaquil went out of the tent, the peeve nosing at her heels, its leash trailing.

"What have you done?" she said to it. "Have you become a strategist? A social manipulator? What?"

"Wet," said the peeve, pleased. It sat in a puddle.

The sound had grown very loud. It was peculiar, as if something tore a thin seam along heaven.

"What's that?" said one of Lizra's captains. He pointed.

They all stared up, into the blue afternoon sky.

Tanaquil was frightened. At once. Not knowing yet why. But something like tea leaves was stirring round and round in the soft, warm clouds. Tea leaves, which made patterns that you could not read, and which grew larger.

Something landed with a plop nearby. They turned. There was nothing to see.

About the camp, others were gazing upward. Soldiers stood in amazement.

"Here, Honj," said Mukk, "don't laugh. I think it's a plague of locusts."

"I'm not laughing," said Honj.

The horrible sound was bigger, more immediate. It was not a scream. It was—a series of shorter screams or squeals—or—

The buzzing drone enveloped them, like an engine descending.

One of the captains gave a shout.

Something had fallen on him. He held out his arm.

"By the Empress! Look at this."

They looked.

"It's a bloody mouse—with wings!"

It was. Black and banded with yellow, its wings large and glassy. It sat on the captain's wrist, observing him with round dark eyes. It *squeaked.*

That was the sound. *Squeaking.*

Tanaquil said hoarsely, "Be careful—it—"

At that moment the mouse jumped. Its tail cracked like a whip and the captain cried out in pain. On his cheek appeared a long red weal. It swelled even as they watched.

"It—it *stung* me."

"They do." Tanaquil said directly to Honj: "A magician made them. They're called mousps. A cross, mouse and wasp—"

The mousp, or another, flew at the captain a second time. They all saw. It bit him on the finger with tiny white teeth.

The light darkened.

In utter fear they looked up and saw that the sky was actually falling on them. A sky made of stinging, biting mousps.

Plops and splashes came as the mousps landed in the mud. And then cries and screeches as mousps arrived next to human skin, and bit it and stung it with the lashes of their poisoned tails.

Tanaquil covered her face, and in that instant saw a flash, something hurled away.

She shouted at Honj, "Protect your eyes!"

But he was already dragging her back into Lizra's tent.

Lizra, so immaculate in her red, glanced at them.

"What is it? Can they have dared to attack us?"

"No," said Honj. He stopped. He swatted violently and three mousps sailed down onto the floor. "Cover your head, Lizra," he said.

"Don't call me Lizra."

"Do as I tell you, stupid girl."

Outside, the noises were bad.

But Lizra bloomed into a white fury.

Just then, the mousps streamed in at the opening in the tent, thrusting with their ghastly little mouse paws. They zoomed about the tent room. As they did so, men too rushed in, in an attempt to escape, falling down.

Tanaquil saw in cold horror how their faces and hands were crisscrossed by vicious red stripes, swelling up and making them look curious, foolish, even as they yowled in pain. Their hands were also bright with teeth nips.

"Empress—it's the end—punishment—aah!"

Tanaquil ducked as mousps flew at her. But the peculiar flash came again, and she saw their waspy bodies blown away. The peeve, crouched at her feet, batted with angry paws. The flash came yet again.

Stupidly, she realized. The gift the black unicorn had given them was real and true and still encircled them. Anything that attacked them met an invisible barrier. She and the peeve were safe. No one else.

Honj yelled. "Damn!"

She saw the stripe across his forehead.

And then Lizra went down with a wild scream, crawling under the table of keys, laid there like wedding gifts from her conquered cities.

Honj ripped a rug from a wall. He whirled it around, and mousps sprayed away in a black and yellow buzzing furious shower.

Some had settled on the cheese unicorn. They were tearing at it, eating it, cutely squeaking.

Outside, over the shrieking and howling, came an awesome crash.

Tanaquil caught her breath. She walked to the tent flap and went outside.

In those few minutes, the camp of the Empress-Goddess Lizora Veriam had become a place of chaos and terror. It *was* terrifying.

Riderless horses were plunging through, kicking down the tents as they passed. Men battled insanely, trying to save themselves with pieces of shirt and tablecloth, drawing their swords in vain.

A fire had been upturned, and already had set alight a group of tents. The burning went unchecked and smoke pushed black into a sky that was still dark with falling demons.

Mousps whizzed at Tanaquil. Instinctively she beat them off. But flashes shone and dazzled, and the mousps were cast aside.

She glimpsed the peeve come bounding out. It leaped to catch the mousps. But the very thing that protected it ensured it could not get a grip on them.

Lizra was screaming. Suddenly the whole of the gold tent erupted, and partly crumpled and went down. Priceless trinkets rolled along the slope: books, gems, a head of marble with sea-shell eyes—

A child ran by crying, stung all over. Tanaquil tried to grab it, hoping to bring it inside her own aura of safety, but she could not get hold of it. It was so scared. It dashed away.

Then Honj crawled out of the collapsed tent and stood up next to her. His face was closely marked by stings and swollen up like a balloon. His beauty was no more. He held Lizra in one bitten arm like a bundle of screaming washing.

"Come on," he said to Tanaquil through shapeless lips, "this way."

"Where?"

"Downhill. It's *here* they want."

He pushed her, dragging Lizra, shielding his eyes as best he could with one arm. Mukk and Spedbo surged behind him, cursing and yelping, also unrecognizable in stings, waving their swords, and Mukk, for some reason, an orange.

The camp rushed by, as if the ground itself were in motion. Roaring men cannoned into Tanaquil, and Honj pulled her away. A woman flapping a dishcloth pelted past.

"It's all right for me—they don't hurt me—" Tanaquil tried. Honj ignored her, pulling her on.

The air was thick with mousps.

When they did not attempt to sting or bite her, Tanaquil came against them. They were furry and soft, adorable. She remembered how Lady Mallow had wanted a pair, and the slap of the tail on the glass, and the dripping venom. Worabex had perfected his secret weapon—

Three soldiers diving through a fire tripped Tanaquil. She fell to her knees and a rearing horse pranced over her head. Its coat was dark with stings. She thought of the camel. It had a thick wool coat, could close its eyes and nostrils—

Honj got her up again.

"Look! Look, woman. Do you see?"

His mouth was now so swollen she could scarcely make out what he said.

But then, through the turmoil of running and outcry and smoke and fire and mousps, she saw the hard yellow gold of Sunshine, the unicorn of war, standing up before her on the edge of the hill above the town.

Something odd. The stokers would not go under its belly. And neither, apparently, would the mousps. The area about the unicorn was empty, and by its legs the stokers and a few others huddled, sobbing and swearing, beckoning them to come and be saved, though there was no room.

"It's the stomach they're afraid of," Honj said. "Under there."

"No," said Tanaquil.

"Safest place," mumbled Mukk, and shoved her.

They were pouring forward. Lizra had stopped screaming. Her face was no longer white and pure but red and black with stings, tears, and eye makeup.

The unicorn bulged above them. And the buzzing drew off.

"In," said Honj.

He ran forward, carrying Lizra, hauling Tanaquil. Mukk, Spedbo, and the peeve thundered after them.

Tanaquil—no one else—screamed. And heard her scream like a white ribbon, unfolding down great emptiness forever.

And then she fell. Fell like a bird or a star. Fell through space or time. To silence. Utter, heartless, unkind quiet. *I am dead. This is death.*

A single mousp glanced onto her arm. It had a piece of cheese, and sat eating it like a squirrel, wings folded, tail lax.

She looked at it with hatred and love.

Poor thing. It isn't your fault.

She stroked its fluffy back.

Its black came up from it and filled her eyes.

XII

A sky could be red. With dawn or sunset. Not a red like this. This red was like bad old wine that had been mixed with blood and then smoked over by the pollution of a witch's fire. Huge red clouds seethed in it, going quickly from horizon to horizon, although there was no wind.

What then, if not the wind, made that unpleasant sound? Those *sounds?* A sort of sawing noise that went on and on. Shrill yet blunted squeals that came at regular intervals. They were alarming sounds—yet also irritating, unbearable, like a faulty clock that ticked too loudly and in the wrong way.

It was hot, humid, heavy. Simply to breathe seemed an effort. But she was breathing. She *was* alive.

Tanaquil turned her head. She had been lying against something hard and her neck was cricked.

She saw a shadowy group of people lying propped around her. She recognized them slowly, as if she had to remember them. Mukk and Spedbo. Honj. Lizra. The peeve sat at Lizra's side. It was looking at Lizra.

So that's loyalty! thought Tanaquil bitterly. But there was no room for annoyance. For something had happened.

They had run in under the belly of the gold unicorn, and here they were, presumably elsewhere. For nothing was as it had been. The landscape, Lizra's war camp, even the unicorn itself—were gone.

This land was very dark. In a sort of red-black twilight, through which one could see fuzzy outlines of distant things, perhaps hills, and over there a wettish marshy region, where pocks of slimy water caught and reflected the revolting sky. The smell of decay seemed to come from there, and so did the mechanical squeals. What made them? Did she actually want to know?

Tanaquil sat up. To her horror she saw something small, black, and yellow lying in her lap. It was a mousp. It was—asleep. It had curled up in her dress and wrapped its tail over its nose. A demon of sorcerous invention, it looked delightful. The perfect small pet. There was just the one that she could see. For some reason it had followed them, the only mousp stupid enough to do so.

For, under the belly of the unicorn, Tanaquil now grasped, lay the gate to another world. She could reason this quickly because she had gone through just such a gate once before. But that had been the entry to Paradise. And this—

It was her own fault. She had mended the unicorn and put into it the earring from her left ear. Obviously the earring had remained what it had been before, a key of unlocking. She had opened the way. And all those men who had disappeared had, evidently, fallen into this place as she now had.

And what was this place?

The other had been Heaven, flawless, wonderful. But there were other worlds, and they said, did they not, the sorceress and mages who talked about such things, that although their world was imperfect, there were plenty far worse.

Who could doubt—that sky, those noises, the prickly, hot, damp, ominous feeling of the red air—that this world was one of the worst kind. One of a variety of hells.

But, if they had come through the gate, the gate should be visible somewhere near.

Tanaquil picked up the mousp and put it on a rock. She got up, and the others looked at her as if she were daft. She turned slowly round and round, staring. Was it the murk that obscured her view? They had fallen, and so was the gate in the *sky?*

She stared. She stared until her head ached and drops of the foul atmosphere beaded her lashes and went stinging into her eyes.

Mukk said sullenly, "There's no way out. We're done for."

Tanaquil glanced at him. "You understand what's happened?"

"Course," said Mukk. "Every kid knows about the other worlds. Half the fairy stories they tell you in the cradle are about them. We've got into one and there's no way back. Should be a gate, shouldn't there, like the way in. Well it's vanished. Here we are."

Tanaquil thought, in desolate rage, I believed only my mother and magicians knew! She led me to think—And stopped herself, since petty anger was too exhausting.

She sat on a rock. The ground was all rocks of many black unlovely types. No grass grew, there was no tree, no plant of any kind that she could make out. Moisture ran over things like sweat. The clouds blew.

The mousp had woken and was washing its face with its paws. Spedbo said, "That thing—shall I kill it, Honj?"

Honj said, "Leave it alone. There's only one and it seems to be in love with Tanaquil." He turned to Lizra, who was still lying, inert, against her rock. "Empress, I'm afraid I've led you into something vile. Do you want me to fall on my sword?"

Lizra did not answer. Her face, with its mosaic of stings and skin and eye makeup run with tears, looked grotesque, not foolish like the stung faces of Spedbo, Mukk, and Honj.

The peeve climbed up into Lizra's lap.

Lizra stroked it absently, glaring away at nothing.

Mukk said, "Be better for all of us. To die here and now."

Tanaquil said, "Don't talk rubbish. There'll be a way out. There has to be."

"It's all right for you," said Spedbo, "bloody witch. You didn't even get stung. It hurts, I can tell you."

"I apologize for not getting stung. But the swellings are already starting to go down. You should have seen what you looked like before."

"Here you just watch it. I don't need some bit of a girl—"

"Shut up," said Honj. He too got to his feet. "We've all had a rest. I suggest, since our sorceress says there's no gate here, that we start to look for one. Or for something. If we're stuck here, we have to survive." Mukk grunted. "That means you too, Mukk. We can't afford to lose a man. God knows what life there is here, but judging by the remainder of it, it must be fairly repulsive, and probably damned dangerous."

As if it heard, something began to hoot up on the vague black hills. Its monotonous voice was added to the other chorus of squealing and sawing.

The mousp flew suddenly into the air.

Mukk and Spedbo leaped up, colliding and cursing, drawing their swords. But the mousp landed on Tanaquil's shoulder, and sat there, looking abominably cute.

"Madam," said Honj to Lizra, "may I assist you to rise?"

Without speaking, Lizra held out her hand. The peeve jumped down, and Lizra stood. She pushed Honj's hand away. She raised her head and said, melodramatically and frankly, "I have lost everything."

"I'll try, Madam," said Honj, "to restore you to your lands and title. Your sister will help. Her magic—"

"My sister," said Lizra.

She gazed into infinity and only looked down when the peeve rubbed against her. She caressed it.

Mukk said, "Well, Honj. Where now?"

Honj said, "Perhaps the Lady Tanaquil has some suggestions."

"I don't," said Tanaquil. "I'm as lost you are."

"Then . . . toward those hills," Honj said. "Something may lie behind them. And the other way goes down into that filthy bog."

Lizra moved without a word again, toward the hills, like a doll set going by clockwork. Like . . . the unicorn. Mindless. The peeve trotted beside her, saying, bolsteringly, "Climb hill. Yes."

Honj fell back. He walked by Tanaquil, on her right side—the mousp was on her left shoulder.

"I have to say, I only knew about these other worlds because *she* told me about *you*. I didn't believe it. But I haven't survived this long without learning you have to change your mind pretty quickly now and then. Do you know *anything* about this place?"

"Not a thing. I'm sorry. I'm powerless. I'm a useless sort of a witch, you know. I should have realized. I *sensed*—but I couldn't warn you properly. The unicorn—its whole purpose was wicked and *wrong*. And so that made a gate into somewhere that's wrong as well, and—evil. *Evil.* Can't you feel it?"

"No. But then I'm thick."

She had the urge to hit him, but he might retaliate. She said,

"I think Lizra's finally gone mad. She's like her father was, after the unicorn—the *other* unicorn—attacked him."

"She'll be all right."

"All she needs is a sit down and a cup of tea?" asked Tanaquil sarcastically.

Honj's face was losing its swollen appearance rapidly. The stings stood out in thin scarlet stripes, cheeks, forehead, and neck.

"She's a survivor," said Honj. "All of us, the same."

"Especially Mukk—let's all die here. *Very* bold."

"Dying can be a way of survival, if the odds are too great. I just don't think they are."

"Don't you."

"No. We have you, Tanaquil."

"It's my fault we're here."

"No," he said, "it's mine."

"Let's *not* squabble over whose fault it is."

"Tell me," said Honj, "on your travels, did you sharpen your tongue on a knife every morning?"

"Yes. And every evening too."

Honj laughed.

Ahead, Mukk and Spedbo turned around with irked disapproval. Lizra did not turn. She walked ahead at a slow regular pace, the peeve by her side.

Tanaquil's mousp began playing with a pearl on her dress.

"*It* doesn't seem to mind."

"It has," he said, "faith in you."

"All right. But *please,* Honj—Honj, *don't* put your trust all in me. I told you—I'm lost. I'm useless."

"I trust myself first," he said. "Don't worry. I'll take care of you."

She turned to him. He looked straight ahead. Her heart, even in this domain of red night, had jumped. She had said his name too, which generally she avoided.

Tanaquil blushed deeply, perhaps with shame. Luckily the gloom of hell would hide it.

They walked for hours, or days—it felt like days. She recalled how in the perfect world it had been possible to go on for miles and miles and feel no fatigue. But here you were tired out after a few steps—before you had even started.

A world of tiredness, anger, squabbling, ultimately, of despair. Evil . . . yes, that too. The dirty-smelling air—like old dishrags, stale flower water—the drenching heat. The dark that was not luminous or intriguing.

The hooting thing in the hills had left off by the time they reached them. The party of survivors sat down again to rest. There was no refreshment. They had no food and had found no clean water, no water at all aside from fringes of the marsh that seemed like poison. No trees appeared. There was only rock, and here and there tracts of cindery black stuff that crunched underfoot with a sound that set the teeth on edge.

As they sat below the hills, the red sky went darker and darker. Tanaquil's veins filled with ice.

It was Honj who said, jauntily, "I think it will be sundown."

Sure enough, once the sky was all leaden-pressing black, a terrible thing that must be a moon rose in what was, probably, the east.

It was huge, this moon, a raised hand could not cover it, and pitted all over like a rotten vegetable. In color it was red as blood. It gave a frightful light, brighter perhaps than the twilight of day.

"I don't like this place," said Spedbo. "I'd rather be in the worst place I ever was. That was the dungeon of Lord Spoot. Horrible, that was, and full of rats. But better than here."

"My worst place," said Mukk, "was my dad's cellar. He used to lock me up there when he didn't like me. Which was quite often. Where was your worst, Honj?"

Honj lightly said, "Nowhere's that bad. Even here. Listen, there's a nightingale."

Something had begun to squawk. It passed invisibly overhead, and Tanaquil shuddered.

Lizra did not speak. She sat stroking the peeve over and over.

"Shall we sleep a bit," asked Spedbo, "before we go on?"

"Are you tired?" asked Honj.

"Yes. But not—sleepy. I feel I couldn't sleep unless you hit me over the head."

"I feel like that," said Mukk.

Tanaquil said, "And are you hungry or thirsty?"

"No," said Spedbo. "Should be, I think."

Mukk said, "I feel as if I'd eaten too much. Drunk too much. Already."

Tanaquil remembered the perfect world, where the delicious air had seemed to feed her and she had needed nothing. Here she *wanted* nothing. It would make her sick.

After a few more minutes, they got up and trudged on.

The hills were not steep, but the endless slope was wearing. They seemed made, the hills, of black pumice. Once something rasped from a hole in the hill, and the peeve glanced inquiringly. But it did not go to see.

They reached the top of the hills as the blood-moon was sinking.

The intense blackness came again. And presently they could hardly see each other, let alone any view from the height.

"We'll sleep now," said Honj. "Or we'll try to sleep."

They lay down on the hard ground and tried to sleep.

After what seemed eternity, Mukk said loudly, "I know you're not asleep, Spedbo. No snoring."

"Likewise," said Spedbo.

Honj's voice said, "Close your eyes and pretend."

Tanaquil thought, There can be no gate out of this world. The perfect world allowed visitors, perhaps, sometimes. So it was possible. But this one didn't want us, and it closed the way so we couldn't get out simply because it welcomes what it doesn't want.

No, that sounded too crazy. And yet—

The night throbbed. There came a faint wuffling sound. It was a noise the peeve made occasionally, sleeping.

So the peeve could sleep here. And the mousp had done so—it had crawled into her hair and now slept again, presumably. Sleep then might occur.

But the peeve and the mousp were innocent. Maybe this world refused to notice innocence.

They, however, were corrupted. And Lizra—Lizra was out of her mind. She had been going to be Empress of everything.

Out of the breathing half-silence erupted a grisly howl right on top of them.

Tanaquil scrambled up and heard the upheaval of the others doing the same, the scrape of swords.

Then a voice wailed shrilly, "Don't cut me! It's me! It's me!"

"And who are you?" said Honj.

Tanaquil realized dim light was returning, a foam of red at the edge of the sky.

She saw Honj and Mukk clasping the three struggling men. Two she did not know. The other was the stoker Bump.

XIII

Knew you'd be along," said Bump. "Someone would come. I told Wijel here, and Plip. Just wait and see. They won't leave us. We're useful."

Plip, the soldier, looked doubtful. His mail was a mess and his army cloak was torn in half and hanging in two strips. Bump and Wijel, one of Bump's band, seemed more cheerful.

"Are the others with you?" asked Tanaquil.

"What others? No. Nobody else. We just met up, like, wandering about. Silly to get lost in the first place. Where's the camp then, Lord Prince?"

Honj said, "I'm afraid we've mislaid the camp too."

Spedbo explained: "You've fallen into another world and so have we. The unicorn's belly was the way in. There's no way out, or there might be. Don't argue. Shut your trap. I'm not telling you twice."

Bump, Plip, and Wijel stood in unhappy astonishment.

Plip said, shakily, "It's some trick of those Locusts."

Tanaquil said, "Just believe what you've been told."

The men glanced at her. Bump muttered, "It's that sorceress. She's rumored to be the Empress's sister. Say yes."

"Yes," said Wijel and Plip.

Bump squinted round. "No rescue then." Bump's orange shirt looked only red, and it was torn and sticky. He also had a scraggly beard. So did Plip and Wijel. But then they had all been there some while. Honj, Mukk, and especially Spedbo were becoming in turn bristly.

Bump abruptly elbowed Mukk. "Who's that girl?"

He was gazing at Lizra.

Her eyes slowly focused on him.

Bump said, "Seem to know her from somewhere. Your girlfriend, Mukk?"

Honj said, "You should kneel when you address the Empress."

"Go on," said Bump, "that's not—" His mouth fell open. He did not kneel or show any sign of wanting to kiss the nauseating black ground.

Lizra stood.

She said, "They all desert me." She stared at Honj. "And you will, too. I know. It was all right when I had power and wealth. Then you were interested. But now I'm nothing. A *girl.* You don't like me now, do you, Honj?"

In her ruined dress, her stung face, tangled hair, she looked bizarre more than pathetic.

Honj said, "Madam, you shouldn't judge me by your other friends."

"Don't lie," she said. She turned her back on him and went walking along the top of the hill, aimless and unstoppable.

The peeve set off at her heels, kicking up black dust and sneezing.

Honj glanced at the others. His face was colder than Lizra's had ever been and his eyes now were steel that was not blue but inky black.

"The Empress is naturally distressed," he said. "But we will serve her here, as in the real world. To the limit of our ability and lives."

Tanaquil looked away. She saw over the hills, and below lay a desert of black sand. Somehow she had expected nothing else.

She went after Lizra along the hilltop.

Lizra did not stop when Tanaquil spoke to her. Tanaquil had said, not *Lizra,* but *Empress.*

"Empress. They need you now more than ever."

"Who needs me?"

"Your men. You're their only banner now. All they've got."

Lizra turned and surveyed Tanaquil. The peeve stretched out a paw, licked it—and spat.

"Don't patronize me, Tanaquil."

"Don't patronize *me*, Empress. I'm speaking the truth."

"All right. And, Tanaquil—"

"Yes, Empress?"

"You've never called me Empress before."

"Now I have."

Lizra said again, "All right."

And walked back. She said to Honj, "Please forgive me, Prince. I'm overwrought. Shall we go down? Into that desert?"

"It seems to be the only way," said Honj levelly.

Mukk said, "And just see what was in my shirt!" He held up a huge squashed orange.

They shared the orange as Honj directed, giving most of it to Lizra and Tanaquil. The peeve ate the peel extravagantly, rolling about.

The mousp had attracted Bump's attention, and he went to Tanaquil, asking if he could see her bird. Was it local? Tanaquil said she would advise Bump not to touch the mousp, but it was too late.

Bump reached out and the mousp jumped up and cracked its tail across his hand.

"Ow," said Bump, seeming hurt more spiritually than physically. "It hit me."

He had not been stung.

Tanaquil picked the mousp off her shoulder. It did not try any violence on her, simply sat in her palm, yawning. She gave it a tiny piece of orange.

"It hasn't got a sting," she said.

"Perhaps that's why it followed us," said Spedbo. "Not with the others. An outcast."

He came over and tickled the mousp, which hit him stinglessly and then ran up his arm squeaking.

The peeve had come over too, after more orange, or the mousp. Tanaquil said, "The great diplomat."

The peeve sneezed atrociously and returned to Lizra.

They edged down the black hill and came into the black desert of hell.

*   *   *

The desert stretched from end to end of vision, under the red sky, and a black mist of dust rose from it to cloud further the cloudy day.

Perhaps the segments of orange had refreshed them.

They kept going again for hours—or days.

Bump said: "We were over in a forest."

"You and Wijel and Plip? A forest?" they asked.

"Well, it wasn't trees. Tall poles of stone with spikes sticking out. We called it the forest. We never tried to cross this desert or that marshy bog thing."

"But now you are."

The dire noises of the marsh and hills had gradually died away. Bump said, "Got on your nerves, those noises."

When asked how he and the others had managed for food and drink, Bump said, "Oh, that." Wijel said, "Couldn't fancy anything," though he had eaten some orange. Plip said, "This place gives you some sort of energy. Only it's not nice. I'll tell you now, I've wanted to cross this desert." Bump said, uneasily, "Yes, I did." Wijel said, "It's like someone calling."

Honj said to Tanaquil, "Is it some sort of spell then that we're being drawn into?"

"Probably. Why did you come this way?"

"Tactics. No. Maybe I'm spelled."

He did not seem to care very much. He had been angry in a cool, suppressed way since Lizra had denied him. He did not speak of this. None of them spoke much.

When the sounds began behind them, they took them for more of the nastiness that had gone before. Certainly they were as monotonous. There was a soft hissing and a low mooing and something like a human voice saying over and over, like a screeking wheel: *Ay*-eeve.

Finally Tanaquil looked back.

A shock of horror went through her, but it seemed far away, fright happening to someone else.

"Honj," she cried, "look!"

Everyone turned except Lizra, who simply stood facing the way they had been going, her shoulders slumped.

In the desert of black sand dust, three black, thin figures were shambling after them, waving their arms. They were apparently human, or humanlike. But, as they got close, you saw they had no hair, and on the ends of their arms were only wodges of darkness, not hands.

It was these things that hissed and mooed and went *Ay*-eeve. But how they did it was a mystery. They had no mouths. Nor did they have eyes or noses. They were featureless.

Mukk, Spedbo, and Honj darted forward, Plip running in the rear, all with lifted fists and swords.

Honj reached the creatures first. He shouted at them, and one came flailing up to him, thumped against him in a cloud of smoky dust. Honj struck it, and both its arms sailed off into the air.

They landed in the sand, and the creature, its mooing unaltered, leaned down and somehow became attached to them again.

Mukk and Spedbo were producing much the same effects.

One creature fell in two halves.

Ay-eeve, it went unmelodiously, and joined together again.

Plip now ran the other way.

Honj said, "Back, drop back."

He and the two Locusts moved back, and the blank figures came after them, but not hurrying. Soon they were about the same distance behind that they had been.

"They just pursue," said Tanaquil. "I think—I think they won't come very close if we move."

"Close once is enough," said Mukk.

They went on, walking backwards; only Lizra walked facing the right way.

The sand creatures came after, never catching up, hissing and mooing and *ay*-eeving.

"What are they?" Honj said to Tanaquil.

"I don't—some sort of demon. But weak. I think everything becomes weak here—or else—I don't know—*angry,* perhaps."

"They're not weak," said Spedbo. "See the one I cut in half. And there it is whole again. You can't ask a man to fight things like that."

Lizra said in a flat voice, "There's something ahead."

Honj looked. So did Tanaquil.

"Another of the pole forests."

"It looks like it. The end of the desert, anyway."

They went on, and the sand things followed.

In what might have been ten minutes they came down among the tall poles of black stone, whose iron-looking spikes clawed out several feet above their heads.

The demons came also to the edge of the desert, and there they folded over and sank into the sand.

In the desert was a pool. It boiled and smelled of rancid oil. Stones floated in it, snapping.

But it was as they stood by the pool that this day's—if it was a day—light began to go, and a new sound pulsed to them through the poles, ringing and singing, miles off, blown by a nonexistent wind.

"What is it?" said Lizra, listlessly.

"It could be anything," said Spedbo, "couldn't it? Er, Empress."

"It sounds," said Lizra, "like a battle."

Tanaquil's ears seemed to open deep inside. She too heard it. Through the vast pulse, the tinny notes of trumpets, the trampling rush of hoofs and wheels, the clash of armies on the shore of night—

"Is that where we've been drawn?" said Honj.

Tanaquil said, "The unicorn was the beast of war and the gate to war. It makes a sort of equation. Mathematics and magic are similar. Things *balance.*"

"What do we do?" said Spedbo. "Is it men fighting—or *things?*"

"Tanaquil," said Honj, "what do we do?"

"Don't ask me."

"I *am* asking you."

The noise was fading again, sinking to nothing.

Tanaquil looked into the anger of Honj's face. Behind his controlled rage was ancient pain. She knew then that she loved him.

She said, "We must go on. We are the makers of war. Here it is. We belong to it."

XIV

Where the forest of poles ended, the land seemed to end. It cascaded down, clifflike, into space. Below was a valley.

At first there was only darkness, for the day had finished in the last minutes of their walk. They had had to feel ahead of them with their hands, and had gone into the poles quite often. Honj and Spedbo, moving cautiously ahead, found the land's dangerous brink. As they halted, the blood moon started to lift, below them.

Mukk said, casually, "Here, Honj. I'll swear it didn't rise in that direction yesterday."

No one else commented.

Blood light flooded the plain beneath, and so they saw the vast expanse of a flat wasteland, nothing on it, until suddenly—the ground began to rise up and move.

"Is it an earthquake?" asked Bump.

It was, of a kind, it must be. The earth below was writhing and shifting and poking out into tallnesses and lengths, and then pouring from both sides forward, *inward,* like two opposing things coming together.

Then the moon was high enough that its scarlet rays ran along the valley, and they saw what went on there. It was easy, for they recognized the scene, as they had recognized its sound.

Weapons flashed like jewels in the red glare. Flashed and struck home. The noise, which had faded away, now swelled up again thick and hot in the hot, thick air. Beasts gave a sort of neighing note, and perhaps those were their roiling, sluggish, heavy shapes.

The trumpets mewled. Some portion of the two forces came together at last with a thundering grumble, and even here, now, the ground shook. Gouts of red light, like spills from the moon, leaped and soared and burst.

"They've got cannon," said Spedbo.

"Every modern convenience of war." Honj stared down at the battle. "Tanaquil says we belong to it. What do we think of it?"

"It looks wrong," said Mukk. "Don't ask me why."

Lizra and Tanaquil said nothing. The others again fell silent.

The ground trembled. A sudden giddiness.

Tanaquil spoke: "The cliff is moving."

"I thought it was just me," said Bump. "Thought I was having a turn."

With a sidelong lurch, the top of the cliff on which they stood dropped some twenty feet or more, and they sprawled upon it, bruised, dismayed.

The sky ran overhead, black red-lit.

Tanaquil crawled to the cliff's edge again and peered over. The battle was coming nearer. They were being brought to the battle.

"Well, this is nice," said Mukk.

They were all at the brink, all but Lizra and the peeve, which sat at her side, an animal now of reddish clay sculpted into fur that stood on end. It had not spoken for some time.

Below, by moonlight-of-fire, they saw the colossal armies hack and hew at each other, the lumbering beasts—not horses surely—the seething, *oozing* quality that was not like, Tanaquil reasoned, a battle of the world.

Above, over the face of the moon, raced black swarms of birds with jagged wings. Crows? No—

"See that," said Mukk, nudging Tanaquil.

"Yes. But I can't make it out—"

Something wriggling behind the armies, where perhaps the wagons and the women might have been. But it was not either of these. Things that progressed in strict rhythm, down and *up,* and the light caught something shining for a second, and there, a spray of darkness—

The cliff juddered and bulged forward again. They were again flung down. At the back of them now a gap was opening, leaving the forest of poles behind. Where land had parted from land, wounds of black sand had opened. The peeve gazed at these a moment. It muttered something Tanaquil could not catch, for the cliff made a grinding sound, and the racket of war was louder.

And beyond the battle—was that the sea? It bunched itself away and bounded forward, tidal darkness, but the moon did not gleam on it as it had gleamed on the "water" of the marsh.

They dropped again.

Wijel whimpered. Plip said, "Should we try to go back?"

No one answered. No one tried to escape.

The battle was now near enough that they could tell the shapes of swords and lances, and crossbows firing their terrible glittering bolts. Cannon coughed and everything ignited for a second.

Tanaquil saw what scuttled behind the armies. Two crowds of—were they men?—*digging*. Digging up the soil of the plain. Digging holes.

"They take their grave-makers with them," Honj said.

And then there was a blare of golden flame. On one side. On the other side.

"What's that?"

"It's cannon."

"No. Oh, *look!*"

From the ranks of either army, something came. Two things. The same. They burned under the hell moon. They were the gold of lava, bubbling, and from them thrust long streams of smoke and steam.

"The unicorn," said Tanaquil.

Each was. Each a unicorn of gold. Fifty feet high. Towering and immense and horrible beyond believing.

The lolloped over the tindery ground, and the alien soldiers shrank from them, and where they did not, they fell.

Out into an island of darkness under the fire of the moon, they careered, and came together with a blast of metal, heat, and tumult.

Each screamed. Their cries split the sky.

They were rearing up. The horns locking, the forefeet smiting. Unicorns made of gold fighting in the valley of hell.

Sparks dazzled into the air.

They were black against the moon.

Lizra had come to the cliff's edge. She stood behind Tanaquil, who was on her knees. All of them but Lizra were on their knees, stomachs, or faces.

"The unicorn," said Lizra too.

"Are you proud of it now?" said Tanaquil. "Can you *see* what it is—here? That's why it was the gate."

"It can fight," said Lizra.

Tanaquil gazed up at her. Lizra's face, from which the stings had almost vanished, was flat as a dish.

"What do you mean—it can fight?"

"I don't know," Lizra said.

She knelt down in silence.

The unicorns fought.

The horns ripped and grated with a fearful searing shriek. Plates of metal were scoured from them, revealing underplates of black or apertures of fire.

Again the cliff rumbled, but did not drop any further.

A bolt of lightning shot from the plain, up into the air. The beings of the armies that had been around it were tossed aside. The lightning hit the black roof of sky and went out with a single blink.

Thunder boomed through the core of the land.

Rain fell—upward. Up from the ground. It was not wet. It was muddy, slimy. It clung to them and slipped away.

And then the sea of land, for it was *land,* which had moved in waves, came rushing in from the horizon and swept up into the air. For a moment the hideous moon went almost out, just one red sliver left like a half-closed eye.

The wave crashed down upon the battle on the plain. It spread, it must be, for miles. It blotted out everything. And as it drew again away, the second of the armies was pulled with it.

Men—if they were men—beasts, cannon, weapons of all sorts, kicking and heaving, and spangles of light came and went, and the wave furled back into the land-sea, and they were gone.

"Bone," said the peeve. "Found a bone."

"Leave it," said Tanaquil. Her voice seemed to come from yards off. "Don't touch it."

"Yes, *bone,*" explained the peeve.

She turned so slowly it was like a dream, and there the peeve was, as she had first known it, as she had so often seen it, digging industriously in the black sand.

"*No,* I said."

"Bone! Bone!"

Something came up from the sand.

It was a bone. It was enormous. It was black.

The peeve got this in its jaws, and *dragged.*

Then all of the thing came up.

Honj pushed Tanaquil down. He had forgotten again she was invulnerable. The others were howling.

Out of the sand, sand gushing off from it like fluid, a huge black shadow rose.

It was made, it was true, of bones. Even its beak was bone. Even its enormous rattling wings. But it had scarlet eyes.

It dove straight up into the air, and Tanaquil stupidly understood that this was one of the things that had flown above the battle on the plain.

"Let go, you fool!"

But the peeve, anxiously, determinedly, clung to its prize, claws and teeth and tail. It was carried up in ten seconds into the sky.

Tanaquil sprang to her feet. She held out her useless, inappropriate arms.

The bird of bone was small now, and the peeve was small as a shrew. It clung on. She heard, somehow, its growling through clenched teeth.

The blackness of the sky absorbed them.

She turned back to the others, but how could they help her? They were looking skyward as she had. Lizra was making motions with her arms as if to pull something down. Her teeth were gritted, as the peeve's had been.

On Spedbo's shoulder, the mousp, which had been sleeping in his pocket through everything else, had come out to see. It glanced at Tanaquil with a curious intelligence. She did not care.

There was so much to say, and all of it would do no good. She did not want to say anything.

She sat down on the earth of hell and held her knees in her gripped arms.

"Tanaquil."

"Go away."

"I'm sorry. Look at me. Something else is happening."

She looked, and saw Honj. Who was he? Did he matter? Yes, oh yes—And yet.

Was loss always so simple, so swift?

What did any of them know. They lost their friends, their mothers and fathers, their horses. To them, what was the peeve? Her pet.

Her *pet.*

She could not weep. She felt pain all through her body. And guilt. If she had been quicker, seizing someone's sword, maybe, leaping—

It had been too unexpected for her. She had not thought that she would lose the peeve in such a witless, sudden way.

"All right. What is it?"

"Turn your head. You can see."

She obeyed him, not concerned.

And, not concerned, she saw that the army, the army that was left on the plain, was doing new things.

The grave diggers were methodically burying the dead. The rest were milling here and there. But, through the midst of this, a column of men on their unidentifiable animals, was now riding toward the cliff. And they were close. A stone's throw.

You could see their battle standards now, gold and blood and black. (No other gold. Had both the battle unicorns been swept away?)

The column was led by a golden chariot. The peculiar beasts were in the shafts, and they had burning plumes. Who rode the chariot?

"They're coming here," said Tanaquil, expressionless.

"So they are," said Honj. "What shall we do?"

"We can't do anything. Be polite, I suppose."

"Will they speak our language?" asked Wijel worriedly.

"Yes," said Tanaquil. "Don't ask me why or how I know. Anyway, I might not be right. I wasn't right about—"

Honj said, "It won't suffer. A thing as big as that—it will be very quick."

"You mean the bird will kill the peeve quickly? Oh, good."

He had forgotten too that the peeve, her familiar, was also protected—invulnerable. So had she. Perhaps in any case that gift of the perfect world would not work *here.* It seemed to her she had lost the peeve forever. At best, the bird would drop it, and surely invulnerability could not save it from an impact with the ground.

Honj said, "You couldn't do anything. I couldn't. It was too fast. Besides, how long would any of us live here?"

"The survivor."

He looked off from her, and she became aware, as if she had shut her eyes and then opened them again, that the pageantry of the awful procession was now much nearer.

She could make out the animals drawing the chariots. Yes, they were kind of horse, but huge and cumbersome, more like the rhinoceros she had once seen . . . and they were not handsome like the rhinoceros. They were in some way totally repellent. And they shone, slick as if wet, although the upward rain of mud had stopped.

Behind, in the chariot, a figure that was enormously tall. A battle-helm of gold and black with floating midnight plumes . . .

"It's their king," said Lizra.

She had stood up.

And then the cliff sank evenly and quite slowly down the last of the distance, and the king of the army came riding up to them in his chariot, with his creatures behind him.

They were black. But not black as black—was. Tanaquil, as she traveled, had met black men and women. They were warm and human, and in their veins ran amber life. These things, that seemed neither male nor female, were black like burned-out coal, like something—dead.

However, the king was not black. He was the color of the daylight sky. Dull poisoned *red.*

He had a face, a throat. The rest was smothered in his black armor and his golden ornaments. From his shoulders swung a black cloak that glittered like a shower of jet stones.

His face—was it like a man's? No. Like a skull. And now he raised the golden vizor of the helm and two eyes were there that were not eyes. Black sockets fringed by strange white lashes. And in the sockets little balls of palest light.

He was so near now that Tanaquil could have reached out and touched the "un-horses." She would rather have died.

She drew back three careful steps.

A quietness settled as the procession halted. There was now only the noise of the plain, of the burials and perhaps the celebrations, and a dim roar that must be the land-sea mouthing at the shore.

The person in the chariot spoke. Not to them. Or only to one of them.

"Lizora," he said.

His voice was deep as a well. It was like breaking bricks.

"Lizora Veriam," he said. "I bid you welcome."

And Lizra's voice came, young and smooth.

"Thank you. And whom do I address?"

"I am the Emperor of this place. I take what I want. I wait for nothing. But I have waited for you."

"For me?" said Lizra. She sounded remote, quite in control.

"I have mirrors of sorcery. They show little of your world. But I have glimpsed you. Now you are here."

The Emperor of Hell raised his black gauntleted hand and drew the helmet off his head. He had thick hair made of rusty chains. On his forehead was a torn black star.

Tanaquil started as Lizra walked by her. Lizra's step was sure, her head held high. She did not seem afraid or repulsed. Tanaquil thought, Why would she, she knows him. He is the god of war.

XV

By blood-moonlight, they went over the lands of the Emperor to his palace. Lizra rode beside him in his chariot. To the others nothing was offered, and Tanaquil was glad of it. The idea of mounting and riding one of the "horses" filled her with such horror that she was nearly sick. The pace was slow in any case, and after them spurled the horde of the army. Its noises were not like the sounds of Lizra's march through the world, which had been attended by oaths, laughter, jostles, the occasional distant cry of a child. This had a sludgy undertow. It was like a river, a landslide, moving at the pace of a snail. But it gave them the chance, if they wished, to sightsee the unspeakable land. Its chasms and treeless hillsides, and at last a long, narrow channel with walls of rock, rising high on either side. There was something strange about the rock.

As they were still near to the chariot, they came out of the defile soon after it, and looked across a flat black lawn of shale, at—the palace.

Tanaquil now had a new desire: to avoid at all costs going inside. But there was doubtless no choice.

Honj said, "Charming, isn't it?"

"I don't have words for it."

"*I* do."

In color it was black and red. Little change there. In form it was a sort of high mound, of many stories, cut in irregular positions by extremely long, thin windows, out of which streamed a thin, pale yellow, unwholesome glow. This lit in turn, for the moon was going down, bizarre carvings that covered the palace from its high top to its shadowy lowest story. The carvings represented the black creatures who were the Emperor's subjects, contorted at every comfortless angle possible, arched over, bent double, straining up and crouching down. Even the windows were held in frames of this carving. Even the roof, which took over from the walls without a join.

They advanced into a courtyard with a carved black wall.

The Emperor stepped from his chariot and assisted Lizra to alight. He had removed a gauntlet. What must he be like to touch? Clammy? Dry as bone—or could his skin feel normal? Lizra seemed to think so.

"Enter my house," said the Emperor. "Attendants will clothe you. We will feast to my victory."

"May I ask," said Lizra, "are my companions safe?"

"Wow," said Spedbo, "she remembers us."

"Quite safe," the Emperor said. "They may do as they please. I have no enemies from your world. It is my pleasure to find my enemies here."

Lizra and the Emperor walked through a rounded, somehow pointed, doorway, into the nauseating yellow glow. Black things scurried after them.

Honj said, "I have to stay. No one else has to. Tanaquil, Spedbo, and Mukk will—"

"I'm staying," said Tanaquil.

She felt more alert. Her shock at the peeve's fate lay under her mood like a cold puddle. Was she glad to be diverted by this filthy palace?

Honj accepted her announcement. Mukk and Spedbo said they too would remain.

Bump said, "I don't really—"

Wijel said, "It's just—"

Plip said, "I don't get paid to do this. I'm not even going to *get* any pay."

"Clear off then," said Honj. "Do you see that hill? Stick around up there for a day or two. We may need you."

"Yes, Prince," said Plip. "Might as well. Only I'm not going in *there*."

Honj and his men and Tanaquil watched the other three trail off up the slope into the blackness behind the palace yards. None of the men-things tried to stop them.

"And we stay together," said Honj.

"I wouldn't have it any other way," said Spedbo.

Mukk said, "One of those carved monsters moved."

They glanced. All was frozen darkness, blots of red.

More of the Emperor's "men" went past them, into the palace. On Spedbo's shoulder the mousp cleaned its whiskers.

"Better put that away," said Honj. "They may eat them here."

"I've put it away three times, Honj. Keeps running out again."

"Give it to Tanaquil then."

The mousp gave a squeak and rushed down Spedbo's sleeve, took to the air with a buzz, and flew to Tanaquil's shoulder. She did not dare to stroke its fur. She would start to cry.

"Let's go in," she said. She strode forward, and over the threshold, through a doorway where carvings coiled and craned and hung upside down. As she passed, one winked its black-on-black eye at her. She refused to respond.

Beyond the door was a great hall, black and red like the outside, and carved all over just the same. Lamps burned on carved black pillars. They were as odd as all of it, shaped like the creatures again, and burning down, here one consumed to the waist, there another down to its ankles, and there four burning only at the top of their heads. Smiling candles?

No one was in the hall except the creatures, which ebbed to and fro, in small groups, about a long black carved table. There were no chairs. On the table lay what must be the food of hell.

"Hungry, Honj?" asked Mukk.

"Oh, starving. Just looking at that makes my mouth water."

Spedbo said, "Just looking at that makes me want my mother."

They laughed.

Tanaquil gazed at them in astonishment, and with an abrupt flicker of delight. Even here they were themselves.

Then she looked back at the table. What *was* it?

The platters were made of rubies, certainly, or some incredibly precious crimson stone. The cups were of basalt, volcanic glass. And into the cups was being poured, from black pitchers, a stream of blackness. And on the ruby plates were . . . stones? Rocks? Rubies?

"It'll be fun watching her eat those," said Spedbo.

Honj said, "Don't judge Lizra. She's your Empress."

"I forgot."

"Don't."

Mukk and Spedbo scowled.

It was Tanaquil who laughed now. She felt herself flush and for a moment believed that there was a way out of it all. But then she recalled the bird of bone pulling the peeve into the sky of night.

The mousp twitched on her shoulder, fanned its wings, and folded them.

Maybe they waited in the hall for an hour. They had got against a wall, but not too near. Tanaquil's feet had begun to ache.

Then there was a flare of trumpets, gold between black lips, and the Emperor came back. He wore his armor, or different armor, for it was now more gold than black, and a scarlet cloak slashed down his back. Lizra came too, holding his arm.

Now Lizra was a princess in hell.

There were rubies in her black hair. She wore a black dress so stiff it too was like mail.

And then the secret was revealed.

Going to the table, Lizra and the Emperor paused.

Six of the black men-things ran at once toward them. There by the table they went into a type of acrobatic act. Two, by Lizra, positioned themselves. One balanced on the other's back. Four, beside the Emperor, did something similar but more expansively.

Once in place, the creatures began to give off a sort of—glue, or putty. They cemented themselves together. They became static, petrified. They were two highly carved chairs.

"Don't faint," said Honj to Tanaquil.

She said tartly, "I don't faint."

"I was talking to Mukk."

"This whole palace—," yelped Spedbo.

"Quiet. Yes. The whole palace is made of these things stuck to each other. Disgusting. Tut."

"And the lights?" said Tanaquil. "Do they even let themselves
be burned? Perhaps it doesn't hurt."

"Perhaps it doesn't matter," said Honj. "Recall the sand-crea-
tures. Cut bits off them and they join up again."

"The battlefield," said Spedbo, "where they buried them—"

"They'll come up in the morning," said Mukk, "like daisies."

The Emperor and Lizra had sat down.

A deep soundlessness was now in the hall.

Tanaquil frowned, trying to keep Lizra's face in focus. *She isn't
my sister.*

No, not anymore.

The Emperor raised his cup of basalt.

"I drink to my victory."

He drank the black stuff down.

He looked at Lizra.

"Excuse me, my lord. I'm not thirsty."

The Emperor nodded. He reached out for a stone from a plate
of ruby. He lifted it—not to his mouth—but to his left eye. He
fed it in.

His eyelashes are teeth!

Lizra said, "Please forgive me, my lord. I'm not hungry.
Women, as you know, are foolish."

The Emperor said, "You must do exactly as you wish, Lizora."

"Thank you, my lord."

The Emperor said to the hall in his deep, deep voice of break-
ages, "We will have music."

So then the things in the hall began to turn themselves into
musical instruments. They fattened or thinned into gourds and
necks, they pulled strings from themselves and attached them.
Then others played them. The sounds were atrocious. Twanging
and thumping, weird pipings and tinkles.

Tanaquil began to laugh again. She hid her face in Mukk's
shoulder.

"Hush, you silly ginger girl."

"I'm sorry. Oh the God."

Then the Emperor spoke again.

"This music is for you, Lizora. A song."

And Lizra, with her pale dish of a face and rubies in her hair, said, "I'm thrilled, my lord, both by the music and your kindness."

"I will make you," he said, "Empress of this world."

Tanaquil stopped giggling.

Her soul sank through her; she felt it. Could a soul weigh so heavily?

She looked at Lizra's radiant face.

Tanaquil turned and ran out of the hall of hell. She ran into the courtyard and into the black of night before sunrise.

Honj caught up to her somewhere.

"It's what she wants. To be Empress of the World. *Any* world," said Tanaquil. "Its even got a moon—"

"Well, there you go," said Honj. It was not Honj, but Spedbo. "He says we'll go out and wait on the hill. He says, that's best."

The day was coming, revoltingly as usual.

They had waited standing in the hall and now they sat on the bare black hill, under the racing red clouds.

"You realize, don't you," said Spedbo, "their clothes—"

"Were made of the people-things," said Mukk. "Yes."

"And his armor," said Honj, "the Emperor's, was himself. He could change it at will."

Tanaquil did not say Lizra had worn a dress made of people. She tried to think of nothing.

Wijel came over. "Shall we play a game?"

"Oh yes," said Mukk, "let's play beat up the stoker Wijel."

Wijel hurried back to the other part of the hill where Bump and Plip were moodily sitting.

"Something will happen," said Honj, coolly.

No one replied.

About two hours later, something did happen.

The lights that streamed gaseously from the palace below went steadily out.

Tanaquil got to her feet.

She felt choked with appalling fury. For herself. For Honj. For Lizra.

The mousp, which had been seated on her shoulder, flew off and settled on Spedbo. Spedbo looked instead upward.

"There's one of those crow things again."

Tanaquil's whole body knotted in on itself. She stared up into the squashed plum of the sky.

Gruesome and black, the bird of bone flapped over it. How could it fly without feathers or membranes? But then, how did the clouds rush by without wind?

The bird circled high up. It made no sound.

"It's got something—it's a rock. It's going to drop a damn great rock on us!"

Wijel threw himself on the ground. Bump ran off. Plip, like the Locusts, watched the sky.

Then the rock was let go.

It whistled as it came—and made a gobbling noise.

Tanaquil felt herself whirled aside as Honj shunted her from the danger zone. Mukk and Spedbo dived away. Then Honj yelled.

He had been throwing his body back. Now he lunged forward. The rock, which was flailing and furry, crashed into him. It made a loud noise and Honj gave a cry. They separated. They were on the earth, rolling. The rock went in one direction, bowling over and over, and fetched up hard against Tanaquil. Her legs gave way. She fell down next to it, and in the next moment the peeve, hot, and stinking of unlikely substances, floundered into her arms.

"Here," said the peeve. It rolled over again, kicked her accidentally, and licked her nose. "Dropped."

"But how—but how—"

"Bone bird," said the peeve excitedly. It was unhurt. Honj had broken its long fall. "Don't eat peeves," it said. "Wanted for nest. *Soft*. Nothing soft here. Peeve soft. Put in nest. Pniff!" it exclaimed, for emphasis. "Nasty nest. All sharp. Made mess nest. Bone bird angry. Flappity. Bring back. Drop."

"My darling," said Tanaquil. She held it tight. The peeve allowed this for half a minute. Then it bit her gently on the finger.

"Mess nest!" yodeled the peeve, springing away, galloping round and round the hill, tripping up Bump and Wijel. It lifted its leg to water a rock. "Peeve *not* soft."

XVI

When Tanaquil looked round, she saw that almost everyone was staring at something on the ground in the opposite direction. This turned out to be Honj.

He was lying against Mukk, who kneeled over him in silence. Bump spoke first. "Is his Princeship dead?"

"No, I'm not," Honj said.

Tanaquil walked over and also stared at him. Even in the red gloom, his face was gray. He lay straight but for one arm, his right, his sword arm, which, very obviously, was badly broken.

"I'm so sorry. You saved the peeve and—"

"And it smashed my arm. Oh dear."

Spedbo said, "You shouldn't have done it, Honj."

Honj closed his eyes. "Well I did."

"I know it talks," said Spedbo, "but she could have got another one."

Tanaquil wanted to hit him. But he was anxious for his leader. Mukk was too. He was gnawing his lip, easing Honj over so that his weight was off the damaged arm.

"It's his sword arm," said Mukk. He gaped up at Tanaquil.

"I know. I realize it's as bad as it could be."

Honj opened his eyes. In his gray face they looked now utterly black. "But that doesn't matter," Honj said. "Tanaquil is a sorceress who can mend things. Lizra told me. She mended the unicorn, after all. Now she can mend my arm."

"Oh—*no*—" said Tanaquil, feeling herself go gray in turn. "It isn't the same—"

"Why not? A broken cog, a broken hinge, a broken bone. Come on. Mend me."

Everyone of them stared at her. She felt alone. She was. These friends of hers might set on her, attack her. It was, of course, her fault.

But she was helpless. They did not understand.

She would do anything for him. She wished she were a powerful witch who could reverse time and undo what had happened, but then, the peeve might have been lost—That would have been no good either.

"I'm afraid," she said sternly, "I don't even know how to set your arm. Surely, Spedbo, you or Mukk—"

Silence again.

Honj quietly said, "Tanaquil, I'm in agony. Do something for God's sake."

"You think I'm something I'm not."

"And you think *I* am. I'll be a cripple. I'll lose everything I have. I'll be a beggar on the streets of some city, unable to take a trade. I only know one trade anyway."

"But," she said, "we may die *here*."

"I don't want to die like this. *Broken*."

"All right," she said. "I'll show you. It will make it worse, me blundering about, hurting you—Do you want that?"

"You'll put it right," he said. He watched her. Suddenly he smiled, grayly, encouragingly. "Come on, sweetheart. Just try."

A bitter taste was in her mouth. Her blood drummed and she could barely see. The hill swung dizzily.

She went closer to him and kneeled down, facing Mukk. She lifted her hands to her face and gazed down at the broken arm. It looked so bad. She had never seen a fresh injury so evident, not even in the war, when things had been hidden from her, because she was a lady.

And it was a foolish injury, not even honorable, though to her it meant so much.

She would do anything—anything—she felt she would give her own life to make him whole again.

She swallowed her own sickness, leaned forward, and put the tips of her fingers—soft, barely there—on the ruin of his arm.

He flinched. He said at once, reassuring her, "Go ahead. I trust you."

That's more than I do, she thought.

And then her hands seemed to move of themselves. In a blazing moment of horror she felt herself clasp him and under her palms the snapped edges of the bone—He made a terrible sound. And she crushed his arm together in a brutal vice.

Honj screamed.

The cry hit heaven above, hit the clouds and fell back on them.

Tanaquil shook her head. She had let go.

Mukk was glaring at her; his once-friendly face, so jokey and gallant in the hall of hell, was raw with hatred.

"You've killed him, you ginger witch. I'll do for you—I'll skin you alive—"

Honj had lost consciousness. His own face was only pale now, ironed of pain by inner darkness.

He lay relaxed.

Tanaquil said, biting back tears, quivering with fear—not of Mukk, but of what she had done—"I warned him."

"I'll throw you off a cliff," said Mukk. "I'll throw you to one of those bird-things—you—"

"Here," said Spedbo, "shut up, Mukk. She did her best. He's not dead. Look, you can see him breathe. Nice steady deep breaths."

Mukk looked. He cleared his throat.

He said to Tanaquil gruffly, "Just get away. Leave him alone."

Tanaquil tried to get up but her legs were water. She said in her mother's voice: "Who do you think you are talking to?"

Mukk glared again and said, "Some—"

And just then, Honj's arm, the right one, snaked up and caught Mukk by his hair and shook him like a toy.

Mukk fell flat on the ground.

Spedbo swore.

Honj, eyes open wide and bright blue, sat up. He grinned. To Tanaquil he said, "I told you you could do it." And he used the right arm again, hooking his right hand behind her head to draw her face forward to his. He kissed her light as feather on her mouth, and let her go.

Then he got up, and standing like a beautiful statue on that hell hill, he drew his sword in his right hand and whirled it round and round.

"I was always strong," he said. "Not like this. The strength in my arm now—I could cut my way through stone and steel. What a repair. Better than new."

Tanaquil lowered her head so her tears could fall unseen on the rock. She allowed herself five or six of them. And then she blinked and rose to her feet as well.

Bump and Spedbo and Mukk were flinging their arms around Honj. Wijel was jumping up and down. Plip said, "We'd have been in a pickle without him, that's for sure."

The peeve sat washing itself, only looking up now and then, in a complacent way.

Mukk came to Tanaquil. "I beg your pardon. Didn't mean it. It was just—you know."

"Yes," she said.

She walked away from them, to the brink of the hill, and stood with her back to them all.

What am I? What have I done? What can I do?

She gazed sightless down the hill toward the palace.

So strangled with feelings she was, elation, fright, distress, happiness—and, somehow, loss. For something had gone from her. Not in the healing but in the triumph and the knowledge of what she had been able to accomplish.

And . . . she had healed *him.* And . . . he had kissed her.

She saw, without seeing, the dark lump of the palace below and an avenue of black thorns that had come springing up in a sort of pathway, out of the valley, up onto the hill.

The black thorns—

Which thorns?

Tanaquil's eyes cleared and she looked very hard.

They were briars, black and clawed, and all around were other dark plants, types of nettles and rank weeds, and there a group of sallow funguses—

"Here," said Spedbo, who had sidled up to her, "what the hell's that?"

"That's what it isn't," she said slowly. "I think—I know. It's us. Somehow—once I was somewhere perfect, and my footsteps destroyed the flowers. But here—we've brought life, at least of a sort. Nothing really attractive or especially kind, but still something *alive*. It's where we walked—perhaps everywhere we've been . . . but we never stopped to notice—"

The others came. (All but the washing peeve, busily snorting and disgustingly sucking bits of fur.) The mousp sat on Spedbo's shoulder.

They looked over and down at the path of thorns that stretched all the way to the darkened palace of the Emperor of Hell.

And as they looked, they beheld a figure emerge from the unlit doorway, quietly cross the courtyard, and exit through the gap in the wall.

It paused among the thorn groves, and then it turned to follow them toward the hill.

The figure seemed very small. It wore a ripped red dress and had long black hair, empty of jewels.

No one spoke.

Finally Bump could not hold back. "It's *her.*"

"He's thrown her out," said Mukk.

"Or sent her to fetch us," said Spedbo.

Honj said nothing. He stood glorious, maybe too full of well-being now to experience rage or embarrassment.

Tanaquil thought, She looks tiny. She and I wear the same clothes and yet—somehow I always think of her as shorter and slighter. She's younger, by a little. About a year. My little sister. Why is she walking toward us?

Lizra moved steadily up the hill. Her pace was quite quick. She did not hesitate, even when she saw them, and when at last she came up on to the hilltop, they split aside to let her pass. Then she stood on the hill and said, "The peeve came back. I'm so glad." She sounded queenly, well-mannered, miles away.

Honj said, and he was cold as ice, "To what do we owe this visit, Madam?"

"I'm here to go home with you," she said. "Of course."

They looked at her.

Mukk said coarsely, "You went off with old Red-Face. There's no 'of course.' Had enough, have you? Or did he?"

Lizra gazed at Mukk, and after a second, his eyes went down. He fidgeted.

"I'll explain," Lizra said, mildly, regal, thoughtful. "I knew you didn't see." She glanced at Tanaquil. "Even Tanaquil didn't. I believed she might. Never mind."

Lizra sat down suddenly on the ground.

They stood around her in a half-circle.

She was a queen who would tell them a story.

Lizra said, "I lived all those years with my father, Zorander. And the Emperor is like my father. He values ritual and power. He doesn't like to be argued with. And his sense of what is right and proper is absolute. I recognized him at once. The armor and the plumes . . . My father. The Emperor. And you see, to a stupid, powerful man, you must never say no. Unless you have a reason he will grasp and can accept. He asked me to be his Empress. I told him my head spun at the honor he did me. I told him it was what I had dreamed of all my life. I told him things like that for—oh, it seemed to be hours. And I listened to his plans. Of conquest, of battle. I used to spend whole days like that with my father. At other times, naturally, he forgot me. I was exactly as I was meant to be. He didn't need to remember."

"So you told Red-Face you'd be his wife," said Mukk.

"No." Lizra glanced at Mukk now, in a kind of faint surprise. "How could I do that? I told him that I longed to be. It was my dearest wish. But that I was prevented. Already I had been be-trothed to a prince in my own world. It was my despair, but what could I do but be faithful? It would be as if, I said to the Emperor, I had been betrothed to him, and then gone off with another."

They waited. Even the mousp on Spedbo's shoulder seemed to be waiting.

Honj said, "He accepted that?"

"Obviously, like my father, he believes in loyalty and honor. These are the mainstays of battle and glory. The processions. The art of *ruling*. To a powerful, stupid man you must never say that you don't want him. That it makes you ill, even to be near him. That he bores and terrifies you. *Never*. He must always be the best. But so must you, to justify his interest in you. And the best is always faithful."

"My God," said Honj. "I thought—"

"I know you did. All of you did. Please," said Lizra, "don't be angry with yourselves that you left me. I've always been alone. I don't expect anything else."

She was blank now. And they—they seethed with shame. Tanaquil felt it. She saw the others also under the lash. Even Wijel. Even Plip.

They *had* deserted her. They had doubted and abandoned.

Tanaquil said, "But are you saying that you thought your father was—stupid?"

"Our father," said Lizra. "He was." She sighed.

Honj said, "Lizra—Madam—what needs to be said must be left for now. You spoke of going home. How can that be?"

"When he knew I couldn't possibly stay with him, he told me how I should leave. It's easy. There's a gate—Tanaquil will tell you about the gates. And now, let me sleep. Just for an hour. He tired me out." She lay down on the hill. She murmured, "He always did—"

Honj went to her and lifted her a little, so that now she lay sleeping in his arms.

The rest of them stood about, like dolls whose machinery had run down. The mousp had retreated into Spedbo's pocket. The peeve, however, trotted over to Tanaquil and sat sturdily on her foot. She smoothed its head.

PART  Four

XVII

Along the river . . .

It was a poem Tanaquil had heard, somewhere. It was about trees on the banks and women washing clothes. This river was not like that.

They had followed Lizra over the hills and suddenly below lay a long gash in the land that gleamed red from the sky. Lizra said, "There's the river. There'll be a boat."

There was. Of a kind.

They stood and marveled at it.

It floated there, anchored or not, against the bank. It was black, but a dry, drained black nearly gray. It appeared to be made of old driftwood, rough and clotted together. But it might be made—of anything. In shape the boat was not like any vessel Tanaquil had seen before. It rose sharply at its center and formed a long, many-humped ridge, from end to end of the craft. There was no sail. Forward, a prow rose. This finished abruptly. It was like a neck— from which the head had gone. Two large oars lay just behind, where its shoulders might have been.

"How does it go?" asked Mukk. "Do we row it?"

"It goes by itself, down to the sea," said Lizra.

"The sea—"

Something ran over the water, dully glittering. It was a little line of fire that vanished with a plop. There was no current in the river, and the water—could it be called water?—was thick and oily.

They followed Lizra again, to the boat. There were handholds in its side, a sort of ladder-thing. One by one they climbed up, Tanaquil and Lizra less easily because of the long gowns they still wore. Pearls tore off Tanaquil's dress as she got over the side and up the slope of the inner ridge. They fell into the water and disappeared. *Must I always leave something behind me?*

The ridge was simpler to ascend and on top of it was smooth between the humps, with scooped places where it was possible, without comfort, to sit. The peeve managed everything beautifully.

Lizra had gone to the front, climbing over all the humps, and Honj and Spedbo went after her. Plip, Wijel, and Bump took the middle. Tanaquil found herself at the back, aft, and Mukk sat down in the next scoop to hers. The peeve climbed a hump and perched, staring.

"Divine," said Mukk. "All we need are wine and strawberries."

The boat started, and by now none of them, not even Wijel, seemed startled.

The oars forward swept back, ahead, and back again, churning the water.

Little streams of fire swirled from them, going out with sticky small glops. The wake of the boat also sprouted fire.

"It's like oil," called Spedbo.

Mukk said, "It's like my granny's soup."

Tanaquil gazed out over the wake. Something moved beneath, rippling in the water, an immense sinuous, scaly something.

"It has a tail too," she said to Mukk.

"For steering, probably." Mukk seemed unconcerned. His main problem was guilt. It was obvious he felt guilty about Lizra, and also about Tanaquil. He had doubted them, and Tanaquil he had threatened, and he had been so very wrong. Lizra was true and pure and clever, and had, perhaps, saved them. Tanaquil was a healer. He kept, therefore, talking to Tanaquil, trying to show how respectful he was, how much he liked her, and how wise he reckoned her to be.

Presently he said, "I wonder about the others. What do you think?"

"The others who came through the unicorn gate? Maybe no one did, they could just have deserted from the army, and everyone assumed they vanished like Bump and Plip and Wijel." She considered how absurdly normal she and Mukk were being, but it was for the best. The tail wiggled in the water, and now, in front, the headless neck was craning left and right. Wijel was pointing at this, but even he seemed resigned. "Then, if others did come through the gate, the Emperor may have sent them away as he has us. Along this river to the sea. Or else—could they have enjoyed this world and wanted to stay? If that happens, perhaps they become . . . like the things here."

Mukk spat in the river. The river flamed brightly for a moment. He apologized to Tanaquil.

The boat glided on. There seemed nothing to say. They were dumb.

Black landscape passed. No trees, no washerwomen. Instead, far off, objects sometimes burned on hills—cities that had been sacked? It looked like that.

The day went, and they moved in blackness except for the currents of fire and the occasional distant light of burning cities. The moon came up. It reflected in the water, and they broke its image as they went.

Mukk fell asleep. He did not snore.

Tanaquil had thought she could never sleep again. You could not, here. But then she did and the peeve curled against her, under the vegetable moon.

"Look, it's a daisy field."

Tanaquil rubbed her eyes, and looked where Mukk was waving. The moon sank behind the land, and against its vivid round lay a place of hillocks. It was a graveyard dug after battle, evidently, for what Mukk had predicted was going on.

From half the hillocks, swords and spears had stuck upward, and elsewhere hands were breaking out. Heads erupted, helmeted, in showers of cinders. Whole bodies crawled and jumped from the earth, fully armed. They made a noise of clanking and scrabbling, a tinny clatter as they juggled their weapons and shields. To the boat they paid no attention.

Once they were free, the sprung warriors began to march away, in a long streamer, off toward one of the distant fires.

"They like fighting," said Mukk, "and it doesn't matter if they die. They come up again. Back to work."

Tanaquil shivered.

Mukk said, "You're very brave, Lady, er, Tanaquil. Most girls I know would be carrying on."

Tanaquil smiled. "I'm past carrying on."

"Do you think we'll get back?" he asked.

"Lizra said so."

"Oh, then. Well. She'll be right." The moon plummeted. It was black. Mukk said, "No one will believe this, will they?"

"I doubt it."

"Just look at him," said Mukk proudly, indicating Honj sitting ahead, elegant, in the shadow of the fires. "Good as new. *Better,* like he said. That was wonderful, what you did. I've never seen real first-class sorcery before."

Tanaquil pretended she had fallen asleep again.

Mukk shut up.

The peeve was aft, on the last hump, scrutinizing the boat's wake. It had discovered the tail.

"Snake!"

"No. Come here and sit down."

"*Big* snake."

"Yes, too big for you."

The peeve glanced at her. It said, "Won't jump. Just watch."

It had begun to explain to her, proper explanations that showed it had listened and understood what she said. She recalled how it had named Lizra a goddess in that unfortunate but well-timed moment of diplomacy. It was learning to be intelligent, sympathetic. Or did she only imagine this? The fond pet owner.

Something stood over the river. Day was coming back, and after a minute, Tanaquil realized the object was a bridge. A bridge built up from the two sides of the bank. The architecture, if so it could be called, was different on each side, but the material was of the dark gray driftwood type, like the boat. The sides of the bridge had never met. In the water hung weapons, not sinking. A cannon lay upended, rusting, on the left-hand bank.

"Two armies," said Mukk, "building the bridge to get together and fight. But they'd already started, and then—they lost interest, found a better fight, died, came up, and forgot."

The tail swished in the water and the peeve chattered its teeth. But it stayed seated.

Tanaquil could hear a sound. It came through the great silence like a silver thread. High and thin, whining. A dreadful sort of song on three or four notes.

"Is that my ears?" said Mukk.

"I can hear it too."

The river was curving a little. As the boat followed this curve, the sound grew louder.

Everyone but Lizra reacted to it. The peeve growled. Even the mousp flew up from Spedbo's shoulder, and then down again.

As the curve straightened out once more, they saw the thing, which stood in the river and sang.

"It's a windmill," said Mukk.

Spedbo shouted over to them, "Hey, it's water mill."

A hundred feet high or more, ink black, it rose into the red sky. But there was a great fanning of black sails. They whirled around, slowed, came down into the water, passed under it, came up again, scattering droplets of fire, pulled slowly upward, and went off into another fierce whirling. It was the action of these sails or this wheel that produced the thing's weird "song."

There was only a slight disturbance in the river. Pools of flame, a brief current.

The boat went on, came under the shade of the mill tower, under the revolving shade of the spiderlike sail-wheel. The sound was very intense, hurting the ears.

But they passed, and the tower slid behind them, and the sound faded.

Ahead now a mist was rising. It was gray. It closed in on them. It reeked of smoke, of ruin, of cold dead places.

Gradually the banks melted into the mist; the fires on the river dimmed to a faint shimmer of pink.

"Where are we now?"

"Sit still," said Tanaquil. "I don't know."

The peeve came back to her, leaving the fascination of the

boat's tail. It got into her lap. It put its pointed face under her arm.

Specters moved in the mist. They seemed like figures, human, wandering there.

Tanaquil saw a little girl, almost transparent as glass, but her hair was red. Her own self, a child.

Wijel whimpered. "There's my uncle."

"Can't be," said Bump.

"He passed away," said Wijel.

Tanaquil thought, Is this a spot where we see the dead—even our dead selves?

It was.

Lizra was standing up. Her white face, from which all mark of the stings had gone, was turned to the right bank.

Tanaquil looked. Her heart changed to lead.

Zorander was there. Zorander, their father, in his cloak of furs and skins, his black hair curling. He looked solid, only a man seen through smoke. And beside him, not quite so clear, his favorite, the wicked Gasb, in a hat that was made like a bird of bone.

Lizra did not cry out. She looked. She saw him. Honj had risen too, but did not speak. Spedbo had drawn his sword, and the mousp perched there on its hilt.

Zorander made no sign. Even Gasb did not sneer.

They stayed immobile, and the boat left them behind.

Do the dead come here?

No—no, never!

Never.

Illusion, that was all. An area of sorcery.

Zorander was gone; Gasb was gone.

Mukk said, "Who was that man? A king? Was it—her father?"

"Yes."

"Poor kid," said Mukk, "I mean, Empress."

The mist breathed thick as night now, and hardly anything was to be seen. For Tanaquil, the other end of the boat, Lizra and Honj, Spedbo, Wijel, disappeared. The other way she could see no farther than the edge of the last aft hump. Not even the flicker of the tail.

Yet they moved on.

The river of death, she thought.

Mukk blew into the mist. He began to sing loudly.

"Oh, when we went to the city, the girls were ever so pretty, but I lost my money and I lost my boots, and I think that's a rare old pity."

Tanaquil laughed.

Mukk laughed.

From up the boat in the mist, the others, but not Lizra, were laughing too.

Tanaquil wished Lizra had laughed.

Then something swarmed up in the mist, a huge black cliff of a thing, and the boat glided effortlessly to avoid it.

"That's a ship," said Mukk, pleased with himself.

They floated under it, and now Tanaquil saw a carven side, all faces and contorted bodies, and a hole blown there.

The mist tattered. They could see through. They were in a forest of slain ships. Ships made of the black and red creatures of this world which, for some reason, had stayed compacted.

Sails dipped, rent banners. There was fire, ships that were in flames, and that gave off the foul yellow light of the Emperor's banquet hall. Where the flame dropped in the water—the water gave way in huge plug holes.

It was no longer, the water, dark and oily. No longer granny's soup. Now it was a gray and lumpy *stew*.

Tanaquil looked at the sick-making liquid. "This is the sea."

The mist had all drawn off, and from the ships that burned there came no smoke.

The horizon was wide, turgid gray.

Yes, they had reached the sea of hell.

Where now?

But there was no need to ask.

Up from the waveless ocean there stood an image familiar now as a recurring nightmare. A fifty-foot unicorn.

It was stopped. It was old and wrecked. Its gold was gone. And as if, even here, it had been made of iron, now it rusted.

Yet it poised there, purposeful, against the clouds, halfway up its legs in the sea.

There was just room. Just space. To go under its belly.
It was the gate.

They could not go through. The boat approached, and ceased to
move. From the mouth of the gate there began to come a hard,
low wind. It blew against them. It meant to push them away.

Under the belly of the unicorn was nothing. No hint of anything beyond. No view even of the sky or sea of hell. No air, it
seemed. A shifting, formless emptiness.

The boat started to slip back, away. Its neck had gone down,
into the water.

Honj leaped up onto the most forward hump. He made a grab
for the unicorn's near hind leg. Got it. With his right arm he
encircled the leg, and Spedbo weighted him to the boat, gripping
the side, face creased with strain. Honj looked only defiant. If
there had been any doubt that his right arm now possessed un-
usual strength, there could be so no longer. Three men perhaps
could have held them there. Honj did it alone.

He shouted at Tanaquil.

He always thinks I know. But then I do.

She gazed up the length of the unicorn's rusty side, and there,
against its flank, she saw a strange whorled hole. In her right ear
the earring that was a key hung heavy as a stone. She could not
reach. She would have to throw—But the gate would grab for
the key. It would not be hard. She drew the earring off. She
glanced at it. Another thing that had been hers, left behind. She
raised her arm and tossed the white fossil into the air, careless,
almost idly. And the wind from the gate-mouth reversed itself.
It drew inward, one vast sucking breath.

A dot of white, the key flew home into the gate.

The boat bucked under them. The tail thrashed in the water. A
wave poured over them, drenching them in the dirty, treacly fluid.

There was no time. Tanaquil shouted so loudly that her voice
cracked: "We'll have to jump. Through under the belly!"

She saw Honj hauling the boat closer to the leg by use of his
healed right arm, and then Spedbo had Lizra and they were racing
forward, dashing off as if he meant to drown both of them in

the unthinkable sea. But as they sailed in under the belly—they were gone.

Honj roared: "Come *on!*"

Plip forced Bump and Wijel forward. They went off, floundering and splashing, vanishing—Mukk was dragging Tanaquil now, and the peeve, or she and the peeve were dragging him. "Let go, Honj. Jump!" howled Mukk. And Honj sprang free and came with them.

They were in air. They were in nowhere. The hell world burst like a rotten fruit.

XVIII

They were in the sea. It smelled of fish and health and light. It was not deep. The sun was shining, turning the air to crystal. The sky was blue as a jewel. The sea was made of blue tears.

Mukk helped her onto a silky beach. The peeve thumped from her arm and shook itself vigorously.

"Tanaquil," said Mukk, wet through as she was, with seaweed hair, "I know I'm only a soldier, but I reckon I can do fairly well. Are you courting?"

She gawped at him amazed. She remembered Gork in the desert caravan, who had made her this offer, and how she had fluttered and lied, saying that she was. And it came to Tanaquil that Lizra had done with the Emperor of hell exactly what she had done with Gork. You did not say no to a powerful and stupid man. But Mukk was not powerful, and he was not stupid. She could be honest.

"Mukk, it's lovely of you. But I can't. I'm not—I've got too many things I have to do."

"Fair enough," said Mukk. He looked sorry and relieved.

Honj was carrying Lizra out of the surf like a prince in a fairy tale. Lizra seemed cool and collected, expecting nothing else. After all, she was an Empress again.

They were in the world. *Their* world.

Spedbo, Bump, Wijel, and Plip were doing a sort of dance, throwing sand at each other, screaming with laughter. The mousp flew over them, hitting them with its tail.

Tanaquil saw what was in the sea.

It was a unicorn. A mechanical unicorn made of gold. In places the plates had fallen off. Then the black iron showed. Around its neck were about forty withered garlands. It was knee-deep in the blue water.

They had come out under its belly. It was the unicorn named Sunshine. The war machine of the Empress.

"Where are you going?" said Mukk.

"Mukk—do you think you could lift me up? Up where that panel is in the side?"

"Course I can lift you. You don't weigh more than a cat. Less than that fat peevy beast."

They balanced in the sea, and Bump and Wijel made fun of them, shouting from the beach.

Tanaquil managed to pry off the panel, breaking all her nails, although it had come loose. She put her hands into the unicorn and pulled out the first key, the white fossil earring that had hung from her left ear. It came without resistance. Then Mukk lost his footing, and they both landed in the water.

On the beach again, at her direction, Mukk beat the fossil into dust with the hilt of his sword.

The grains scattered in a soft breeze.

Soon after that, the scouting party from the army, Lizra's army, came down the dunes and arrested them. Then Lizra got to her feet and stared at the party captain, and he went green and crashed to his knees.

"Empress!"

"Why are you here?" she said, cold as the sweet white snow that would fall in the world, clear as the clear water of its rivers.

"We kept on to the sea, Madam. Your last orders before you were taken. Captain Chortal—"

"Who is Captain Chortal?"

"One of your commanders, your Radiance."

"Yes, I believe I recollect him. Well?"

"He took charge of us, Madam. We marched to the sea. And we fired the unicorn to celebrate—and it went right on into the water, Madam. And—we couldn't get it out. But then the sorceress has come back with you. She can help make a new one."

Tanaquil said, "No."

And Lizra said, "You hear correctly, Captain. No. The days of the unicorn are over."

The camp was blissful. It sprawled up and down the slopes of meadows. More time had passed here than had gone by in the world of hell, a month or more. Autumn was leaving the land in gusts of tawny flowers and red trees. A brown river had silver fish in it. The children were playing and quarreling and the women cooking at their fires. The soldiers lazily polished armor or kept going complex dice and card games. Some wrestled, some lay asleep under improvised awnings.

There had been no battles. Every town and city surrendered, hung them with late flowers, gave them wine, wanted to see the unicorn. In the end little children had run out and tied ribbons on its legs. It had become a toy.

The night by the sea, they fired it to show the last villages how it moved. They had aimed it at the water for safety. In the sea it sizzled and its fire went out.

They were sorry to say, seagulls had done things on it. And it was beginning, severely, to rust.

Of the mousp swarm they spoke now with grim amusement. The stings soon went off, no one had suffered more than a day's real inconvenience, even the smallest children who were stung. Having worked havoc, the swarm had flown away. They had not seen it again. Nor, of course, the Empress. They assumed she had been abducted, in the confusion, and that Honj and his two Locusts had gone to rescue her, taking the Lady Tanaquil along to provide magic.

They were so sure of the abduction that nothing needed to be said of the gate into hell. And, indeed, when Bump did boast of it to the stokers, they set on him and gave him two black eyes. The stokers, and the artisans, were not happy. They sensed they were out of a job.

Honj had, naturally, dispatched the abductors of Lizora Veriam. The next step would be for some enormous honor to be awarded him. The rumor was that this would be marriage to the Empress he had saved.

*   *   *

For two hours, Lizora Veriam's counselors and captains, her favorites, her important servants, and hundreds wanting attention, or to see she was really back, trooped through her golden tent, where she sat on her throne in a dress of brilliant green stitched with diamonds. She told them all that the war was now over. Some argued, and she froze them with her eyes. Some seemed rather glad. She announced that from tomorrow there would be feasting for three days and nights to celebrate her return. She smiled on those who had earned it, and pinned on Captain Chortal a medal so heavy he could hardly stand upright.

When everyone had gone, the sun had set, and dusk was washing peacock blue across the holy, sane, and blessed sky.

Lizora sat in the golden tent and sent the last of her following away, except for Tanaquil and Honj, Spedbo and Mukk.

She offered the Locusts then great fortunes, which all three meekly accepted, even Honj, looking sheepish.

Tanaquil laughed.

"And for my sister," said Lizra, "what?"

"Just forgive me."

"If *you* will."

And then Lizra's face crumpled. She was crushed together and became a tiny child in a silly, too-ornamental dress that scratched. She stared at Honj and began to cry, messily, frantically. She wailed in a high, lost voice, "I want my daddy—I want my daddy—"

And Honj went to her and held her, and Mukk and Spedbo and Tanaquil crept from the tent, and stood on a hillock and told each other how wonderful the night smelled, and what joy it would be to be rich, until the two men slunk off to find their comrades.

And then Tanaquil stood in the dusk above the human camp, alone.

She could smell the wonderful night, all dropped leaves, the sea, the water of the brown river, flowers, suppers, horses, goats, and earth, sheer earth. And she could hear the babies and the songs of women and the guffaws of men and the bark of dogs.

The mousp had stayed with her and sat in a patch of clover, preening. They had had to reassure, over and over, that it had no sting. The peeve was trying to catch the evening moths that had been drawn to the lamps, but really it did not care and finally rolled over and lay there, like a fur barrel, with all four legs sticking up.

I came from heaven with a gift. I came from hell with something lost.

She did not think he would come out to her, not really. Yet she knew that he would.

The sky was black by then, diamond-sewn with stars, and with a high white moon.

He said, "She's asleep. That serving woman who's all right is watching her."

Tanaquil said, "She'll be better for crying. She had to do it all in the end. She always has. It's too much."

Honj took Tanaquil's hand, held it a moment, then gave it back to her. He said, "I can't leave her."

"She'll make you an emperor."

"Just what I want. To get fat in some palace. God help me."

"I can't see you fat," Tanaquil said.

"She wanted to dismantle the empire. Give every city back its freedom. I had to tell her she couldn't do that now. That it would be taken for weakness. She's given them ideas. Someone else will start out to conquer the world, and we'll be at war again. No, she has to rule what she's got and rule it damned well. Nothing else anyway will satisfy her. She's a perfectionist."

"Yes. But she'll have you."

"You," he said, "have that."

She turned and stared up into his face. Against the glory of the night of earth, he seemed now only pleasing, almost ordinary. She hurt with love. She said, "Thank you. But I shall go away."

"Go far away," he said. "Please."

They stood, and the moon moved. In the grass the peeve snored and the mousp had made a sort of nest, unnoticed, in its tail.

"One thing," he said. "Will you give me that little silver ring you wear?" She slipped it from her finger—Mallow's gift. It did not fit him; his hands were too large. He said, "I'll keep it anyway."

"I'll think of you sometimes," she said, "keeping my ring. But only now and then. It must only be now and then."

He looked at her. He touched her face with one finger. Then he went back into the golden tent, to his Empress and his wife.

XIX

Going home. Home to her mother's fortress in the desert. A long journey still. And plenty to think about. Yet Tanaquil rode in a daze. The canny camel took care of her. It had even greeted her in the camp with a kind of welcoming noise. An old friend. She was glad of it, and of the peeve, which every new day went quite mad, reveling in the world. The mousp still puzzled her. Her mother would doubtless find it interesting.

Mostly, mostly, she thought—she thought of Honj, despite what she had declared. She remembered everything he had said and done. It was all she had of him. She had lost the rest.

She did not think of his future wedding to Lizra. When she thought of Lizra, she did so carefully, separately. They had parted warmly, a false, showy warmth with one awkward hug—like the last time. Good-bye.

She had lost Lizra too. For if her sister was to be Honj's wife, then they could never meet again.

And Lizra had given her a necklace of emeralds. Green for youth. Tanaquil had never grasped that it could be possible to hate a necklace. And then, she thought, she could give the emeralds to her mother, Jaive, who would look marvelous in them, and everything was all right.

She had never felt such sadness. Yet the sharpest pain died away as the days went past. The sadness became almost restful. It was so known.

And she began to consider, too, her mother. For what would Jaive be like? How would she act? What had happened to Jaive since Tanaquil left her?

Six weeks after she had gone from the camp, up in some fragrant green hills where cedars grew, they stopped for the night beside a stream, and Tanaquil spent a whole hour gazing at this stream, as now she often spent hours gazing at green leaves on blue sky, or birds flying.

She had gained something after all. The perfect world had made her see the worth of this one. Now she truly beheld this one's loveliness. It's *goodness.*

The mousp, when she came from the stream to make her fire, had disappeared. This happened occasionally. It always came back. She had assumed it went to gather food of some sort, but had never discovered, beyond cheese—which she fed it—what it liked.

The camel was browsing on the cedars, for it was always experimenting. The peeve was chasing rabbits, never catching them, with wild squawks.

Tanaquil laid the first stick, and a shadow fell across the ground.

She jumped up in alarm.

A man stood there. He was in middle age, but tall and well built, with a cloud of graying black hair and a strong face. Two dark eyes looked at her in a way she found annoying.

"Good evening, Tanaquil," he said. "You won't remember me. Worabex, the magician."

Tanaquil dropped her firewood, more in irritation than surprise.

"I thought you wouldn't change yourself."

"I can do anything I like," he said, arrogantly. "I said to make myself young would be a mistake. But I can present myself with a commanding appearance as well as in the rather short, bald version I save for visitors."

Tanaquil said, "What do you want?"

"A little courtesy, perhaps."

"You're the rude one, appearing from nowhere."

"That's not exactly a fact. You saw me only this evening."

"What a *lie!*"

Worabex smiled insufferably. "I told you you had lessons to learn and you have done extremely well. A talented pupil."

Tanaquil was furious.

She said, "I'm afraid I must ask you leave."

"The night is so wide," he said. "Can't I share a piece of it? I see you still fear my advances. Did it never occur to you that I was interested in you in a—shall I say—*fatherly* way?"

"No."

"I must be frank then. We've been friends for ages. You've even petted me. It was very nice. My fur took on quite a gloss."

"What are you—?" Tanaquil went hot, then cold. She said, in a voice of stone, "The mousp without a sting. A shape-changer. It was you."

"Indeed. And thanks to you, and that helpful mercenary Spedbo, I have done what few of my peers have ever dared, entered and seen *another world.* My gratitude, dear Tanaquil, is overflowing."

"Go away," she said.

"I have other plans. I'm traveling with you. You will find I'm useful. You'll pretend I'm your father."

"I will not."

"And then that way, I shall get to meet your mother, whom I have heard of, and whom, I admit, intrigues me very much. There. You see, I'm actually more interested in a lady of my own age."

The peeve appeared on a nearby hill. Now it was actually playing *with* a rabbit. The rabbit was chasing the peeve.

"I don't want your company," said Tanaquil. "And my mother—I disapprove of your intentions toward *her.* I mean, you'll make her *worse*—"

Worabex laughed, throwing back his head. He looked impressive. Jaive might like him. And he would, he *would* bring out all her qualities of mystic craziness.

The peeve hurtled down the hill, the rabbit in pursuit. The peeve was crying: "Good! Good!" Under the cedars, the camel sidestepped to let them by.

"Then you refuse my company," said Worabex.

"I'm afraid so."

"A harsh daughter. Have you *ever* been kind to your mother at all?"

Tanaquil bristled and the peeve surged by.

Then—Worabex was gone. Something tiny darted like a glint of the fallen sun. A golden *flea.*

The peeve sat and the rabbit stopped in a long, grassy skid, backed away, waiting.

The peeve scratched.

"Itch," it explained. And after a moment, "Flea."

Tanaquil stood on the honey-green hill. Something in her was awake again. She cursed. She *knew*.

Even if the peeve found the flea, it would be the wrong one.